W9-AHU-457

The Ghost of Cutler Creek

Also by Cynthia DeFelice

The Apprenticeship of Lucas Whitaker

Death at Devil's Bridge

The Ghost of Fossil Glen

The Ghost and Mrs. Hobbs

Nowhere to Call Home

Under the Same Sky

The Missing Manatee

Casey in the Bath,
illustrated by Chris L. Demarest

Old Granny and the Bean Thief,
illustrated by Cat Bowman Smith

The Real, True Dulcie Campbell,
illustrated by R. W. Alley

One Potato, Two Potato,
illustrated by Andrea U'Ren

Cynthia DeFelice

The Ghost of Cutler Creek

A Sunburst Book
Farrar, Straus and Giroux

Distributed in Canada by Douglas & McIntyre Ltd.
Printed in the United States of America
First edition, 2004
Sunburst edition, 2006
1 3 5 7 9 10 8 6 4 2

Library of Congress Cataloging-in-Publication Data
DeFelice, Cynthia C.
The ghost of Cutler Creek / Cynthia DeFelice.— 1st ed.
p. cm.
Summary: When Allie is contacted by the ghost of a dog, she and Dub investigate the surly new boy at school and his father to see if they are involved.
ISBN-13: 978-0-374-40004-0 (pbk.)
ISBN-10: 0-374-40004-0 (pbk.)
[1. Ghosts—Fiction. 2. Dogs—Fiction. 3. Family problems—Fiction. 4. Mystery and detective stories—Fiction.] I. Title.

PZ7.D3597 Gf 2004
[Fic]—dc21

2003049051

For Josie, Bogey, Tora,
Enki, Harriet, Jake, and Carrie,
good dogs all

The Ghost of Cutler Creek

One

The whimpering grew louder and more desperate, then rose to a keening wail. Allie Nichols ran down the long, shadowy hallway, trying to reach the source of the sound. The sadness and hopelessness of it tore at her heart. She had to find out who was in such terrible misery. But it was so dark, so difficult to see! She followed the cries through countless twists and turns and found herself at a dead end.

She forced herself to stop and listen, to try to get her bearings. At first she couldn't hear anything but the rasp of her own breath, ragged from running. Then—there! A whimper, but fainter now than before, farther away. She had gone the wrong way!

Racing back, she followed the pitiful sound through the endless corridors. Sometimes she thought it was the cry of a baby; at other times she was sure it was someone older. The next moment it sounded like an animal or a bird. She desperately wanted to help, but first she had to find whoever—or whatever—it was.

Nearly weeping with exhaustion and frustration, she turned a corner, only to reach another dead end. The wail faded to a plaintive whimper and stopped. Now crying, Allie pounded the wall with her fist—and woke up.

She had been beating, not on a wall, but on her pillow. Uncurling the fingers of her fist, she sat up and wiped the tears from her cheeks. Her mind cleared and the foggy wisps of her dream receded, but she was left with a lingering feeling of sorrow.

Along with the sorrow was a sense of excitement—and dread. For Allie knew what the dream meant. Twice before she had wakened from urgent night-mares like this one. Both times the dreams had been messages from someone who wanted her help. Both times that someone had been a ghost.

* * *

When Allie went downstairs to breakfast the following morning, her mother was talking on the phone, a worried expression on her face. One look at her four-year-old brother, Michael, and Allie knew why. His eyes were red and puffy. He glanced up at Allie, sniffled, and exploded in a sneeze.

"Either it's a cold, or his allergies are suddenly acting up," Mrs. Nichols was saying into the phone. "Whichever it is, I'd better get him in to see Dr. Waheed. Could you cover the store for me today? Great. Thanks, Reggie. I'll call you later to see how you're doing. Okay. Thanks again. Bye."

Mrs. Nichols hung up. "Morning, Allie."

"Hi, Mom."

"Can you walk to school this morning?"

"Sure."

"I'm staying home today to take Mike to the doctor."

"I heard." Allie poured herself a bowl of cereal and added milk. Turning to her brother with a sympathetic smile, she said, "Mikey, you don't look so hot."

Michael made an attempt to smile back, but sneezed instead.

Mr. Nichols came into the kitchen, his briefcase in his hand. "Not feeling any better, Mike?" he asked.

Michael shook his head. Then he wrinkled his nose. "Something smells funny. Poopy."

Allie and her parents all sniffed the air.

"I don't smell anything," said Mrs. Nichols.

"Neither do I," said Allie's dad.

For a moment, Allie thought she did catch a whiff of something "poopy." But when she sniffed again, it was gone.

Allie and her parents looked at one another and shrugged.

"I've got to go," said Mr. Nichols. "Smooches all around." He gave Allie and her mother each a kiss. "Except for you, big guy," he said, giving Michael a pat on the head. "If you've got Stinky Nose, I don't want to catch it."

Allie laughed and got up from the table to get ready for school. She called her best friend, Dub Whitwell, to say she was walking, and that she'd meet him at the corner.

As soon as Dub showed up, she told him about her dream.

"Oh, boy," he said. "Here we go again. It sounds as if Allie Nichols, Ghost Magnet, is back in action."

In his voice Allie detected the same combination of fear and excitement she'd felt on awakening from the dream. She nodded, saying, "I think so, too." Then she asked, trying to sound casual, "You did say here *we* go again, right?"

"Of course," answered Dub. "Are you kidding? I wouldn't miss this for anything." He grinned and gave her a snappy salute. "Dub Whitwell, your Faithful but Clueless Companion, reporting for duty."

"What do you mean, *clueless*?" Allie protested.

"You're the one who attracts ghosts, Al," he said.

"I can't see 'em or hear 'em—I just come along and get scared out of my wits."

Allie smiled. Dub had helped her enormously during her two previous ghostly adventures. He was the only other person who knew she saw and heard ghosts, if you didn't count Michael. And Allie didn't, really, because while Michael saw and heard them, he didn't understand that they were ghosts.

"So what now?" Dub asked. "We just wait to see what happens next?"

"I guess so," Allie answered. "There's nothing we can do until we know who the ghost is. And what it wants."

They were passing Luv'n' Pets, the local pet store. As usual, Allie stopped to look at the puppies in the front window. There were new ones every couple of weeks. The last batch of yellow furballs had been replaced with a litter of seven tiny brown-and-white furballs.

"Oooh, look how cute you are!" Allie crooned, sweet-talking the puppies through the plate glass. But this time she was distracted by an unpleasant tingle that ran through her body.

"Oh, Dub!" she cried. "I just had that—that *feeling*. He was back. Or she—or it. Anyway, the *ghost*!" Allie stood still, trying to focus with every fiber of her body. "It's gone now."

"Are you okay?" Dub asked.

Allie collected herself and nodded, but she was feeling a little shaky.

"They never just tell you what's going on, do they?" Dub said. "Every once in a while you get a clue, and you have to go from there."

"Yeah." Allie gave him a wry smile. "Ghosts are funny that way."

Dub glanced quickly at his watch. "We better get moving or we'll be late."

"Bye, puppies," Allie called as she and Dub started walking again. "Hey, speaking of puppies, I thought of something to give Mr. Henry and Hoover for an end-of-the-year present."

Mr. Henry was Allie and Dub's sixth-grade teacher. Hoover was his beloved golden retriever, and the class mascot. It was the next-to-the-last day of school, and, although excited about summer vacation, Allie couldn't bear to think that her days in Mr. Henry's classroom were coming to an end. He was without a doubt her favorite teacher in the world. She was going to miss him—and Hoover—terribly.

"Yeah?" said Dub. "What?"

"Remember Mr. Henry said the vet told him Hoover has to go on a diet? Well, a friend of Mom's made up a recipe for low-calorie, healthy dog biscuits, and Mom found a bone-shaped cookie cutter, so I'm baking some treats for Hoover. And I'm making a collar for Mr. Henry."

"Oh, he'll look terrific in that," said Dub. "Don't forget a matching leash."

"Very funny. I started it last night, and it's turning out pretty good. I'm making it out of red cord, and I'm sewing Hoover's name and phone number in black."

"So guy dogs can see them and call her up for dates?" Dub asked with a grin.

"Right," Allie answered. "Or, if she gets lost, whoever finds her can call Mr. Henry."

"Cool," said Dub.

"Want to come over and help me make the dog treats after school?"

"Okay."

When they walked into their classroom, Allie noticed a boy she had never seen before standing by Mr. Henry's desk. The bell rang, and all the kids found their seats, except for the boy, who continued standing.

"Everybody, I want you to meet L. J. Cutler," Mr. Henry announced. "He'll be with us for the rest of the school year." Here Mr. Henry stopped and smiled. "What's left of it, anyway."

The kids laughed, and Mr. Henry went on. "L.J. came to us all the way from Georgia, and I know you'll make him feel welcome."

Several kids, including Allie and Dub, called out, "Hi, L.J."

Allie heard Karen Laver mutter, "What kind of name is *Eljay*?"

Allie figured *L* and *J* were initials, standing for something else, probably a real name that L.J. didn't use for some reason. Sort of the way "Dub" was short for "double." Dub's real name was the same as his father's, Oliver James Whitwell. Luckily for Dub, his mom had nicknamed her son "Dub" to save him from being called Ollie or Junior.

As usual, Karen had kept her voice just soft enough so Mr. Henry couldn't hear her comment. Allie pretended she hadn't heard, either.

Mr. Henry turned to the new boy and said, "We're glad you're here, L.J. What brings you and your family to Seneca, New York?"

L. J. Cutler looked out from under a shock of tousled brown hair that fell across his eyes. He didn't smile, or look bashful or embarrassed, or do anything Allie might have expected from a new kid standing in front of a group of strangers who were curiously checking him out.

The room was quiet while everyone waited for L.J. to speak. In a low voice he muttered, "What do you want to know for?"

There was a moment of stunned silence. Then Mr.

Henry said, "All right, L.J. I didn't mean to put you on the spot. Why don't you take that empty desk next to Allie. She'll be happy to show you the ropes. Won't you, Allie?"

"Sure," Allie answered automatically. But she wasn't sure at all. She wasn't sure she felt like talking to this strange, surly boy.

L.J. fell into the chair beside her, slid down, stuck his legs straight out in front of him, and folded his arms across his chest. Without looking at her, he said so softly only she could hear, "I don't need you or anybody else for a baby-sitter, so just back off."

For a second, Allie stared at him, dumbfounded. She couldn't believe he had just said something so downright rude. Then she grew angry. Who did he think he was?

"Fine with me," she said shortly, quickly looking away from him. She sat staring straight ahead, her heart racing, outrage at L.J.'s behavior making her pulse beat really fast.

At that moment, the skin on the back of her neck began to prickle, and her hands grew cold and clammy. In her head, the cries and whimpers from her dream echoed pitifully. Her ghost was back. What was it trying to tell her?

Allie could hardly think. It seemed that too much was happening at once. Then, recovering herself, she sent a mental message to the ghost: *Would you hurry up and let me know who you are so I can help you?*

She sent a second mental message, to L.J.: *Back off yourself. I've got enough to worry about without baby-sitting you.*

Two

Allie barely heard a word of the book Mr. Henry was reading to the class that morning. So far, it was a great story, and it was building to an exciting conclusion, but between L.J. and the ghost, there was no way she could relax and listen.

She was almost afraid to look in L.J.'s direction. Actually, she didn't have to look; she could feel him beside her, a dark, threatening cloud at the edge of her vision.

"Allie?"

Uh-oh. Mr. Henry must have asked a question about what he'd been reading, and was now waiting for her answer. She felt her face flush with embarrassment. But to her relief, Mr. Henry continued talking. "Would you please introduce L.J. to Mrs. DeMarsh?"

"What? Oh, sure," she said. She glanced at the

clock, and realized that Mr. Henry must have announced that it was time for music.

The rest of the class began lining up at the door. Quickly, Allie looked at L.J. He was still sitting, as if deciding whether or not he *wanted* to go to music class. Finally he rose and, without a glance at Allie, sauntered over to join the line behind Dub. Allie followed.

"Hey, L.J.," said Dub in his friendly fashion.

Allie winced, and waited to see what L.J. would say. After his comment to her, she wondered what kind of response Dub was going to get.

L.J. gave no indication that Dub had even spoken. With his chin up and his eyes narrowed, he stared toward the door. He wasn't looking at anything or anybody in particular, as far as Allie could tell. He acted as if he were alone, as if the rest of them weren't there.

Dub looked at her, shrugged, and mouthed the words "What's with him?"

Allie made a sympathetic face and shrugged back. The line of kids moved out into the hallway, and Mrs. DeMarsh ushered them into her room. When Allie introduced L.J., Mrs. DeMarsh welcomed him warmly. "But I'm afraid, L.J.," she said, "that this is both hello and goodbye."

She looked at the rest of the class and said sadly, "Today is your last music class at Seneca Heights

School. If I think about it, I just might start to bawl. So let's sing instead. Why don't we do all our old favorites."

Turning back to L.J., she said, "We'll start with one of *your* favorites, L.J. Name it and we'll see if we know it."

L.J. shook his head and looked away.

Allie saw a flicker of surprise pass quickly across Mrs. DeMarsh's face. Allie thought she knew how her music teacher felt. L.J.'s attitude was definitely unsettling.

Allie watched him from the corner of her eye all through music class. He never said a word or sang a note.

Afterward, the class went to lunch. On the way down to the cafeteria, Allie was certain that L.J. was right behind her. As she passed through the line with her tray, she planned to introduce him to Mrs. Hobbs, the cafeteria lady. But when she turned to present L.J., he wasn't there.

Allie joined Dub and some of the other kids from her class at a table, and looked around. "Where's L.J.?" she asked.

Karen Laver said carelessly, "I don't know, and I really don't care. You can move to another table if you want to eat with him. *I* certainly don't."

For once, Allie agreed with Karen. But she wasn't going to say so. She stood up and scanned the lunchroom one more time, but L.J. was nowhere to be seen.

She shrugged and sat down. "Maybe he got sick or something," she said.

"He's probably smoking in the bathroom," said Karen. "Or trying to burn down the school. He seems like the psycho type."

Allie had been the target of Karen's cruel teasing many times herself, so she always stuck up for other victims. Now that Karen was picking on L.J., Allie felt a rush of sympathy for him. "Give him a break, Karen," she said. "It's his first day."

"What is he, your new boyfriend or something?" Karen taunted.

"That is ridiculous, Karen, and you know it!" Allie said. "I've barely said two words to the guy."

"Whatever," Karen said, sounding bored. "Anyway, it looks like he took off. And you were supposed to be watching out for him." She smiled sweetly, adding, "But don't worry. Mr. Henry won't blame you. You're his little pet, after all."

Allie turned away, refusing to get sucked into Karen's stupid games. To the other kids at the table she said, "What I keep wondering is why L.J. bothered coming for the last two days of school."

"Isn't there a law that says kids *have* to go to school?" Joey Fratto asked.

"I think so," Allie said. "But for the final two

days? I mean, it's not like we're going to do any work. Mr. Henry will probably finish reading us the book this afternoon, and tomorrow is the party."

"It does seem dumb," Dub agreed. "That's probably why L.J. left. But you've got to admit, it takes guts to just walk out of school."

When L.J. didn't return to the room after lunch, Mr. Henry asked the class where he was. The kids all shook their heads, and Allie explained that no one had seen him since music class. Mr. Henry picked up the phone and called the office, a worried expression on his face. Then he finished reading the book, and the class spent the rest of the afternoon discussing it. L.J. never returned.

When Mr. Henry dismissed them, the kids reminded him that he had promised to bring Hoover to school for the last-day party.

"You don't think she'd let me leave without her tomorrow, do you?" Mr. Henry asked. "That dog never misses a party if she can help it."

As Allie walked past his desk, Mr. Henry said, "Allie, can you stay for a minute?"

"Sure." She glanced toward Dub and said, "Wait for me, okay?"

Mr. Henry smiled at her. "I was wondering if you might be available to doggy-sit Hoover next week."

Allie didn't even have to think about it. She loved the big shaggy dog, and had watched her once before when Mr. Henry had gone away for a weekend. "You bet!" she answered.

"Great! A friend of mine was supposed to teach a summer seminar at Iowa State, but her son is sick and she can't do it. She's asked me to fill in for her. I'd like to help her out, but only if I can make arrangements for Hoover. If you could take care of her, it would really put my mind at ease."

"I'd love to," Allie said. "Really."

"You're not going to camp or on vacation?"

"Nope. Not until August."

Mr. Henry held up one finger and shook it at her playfully. "And don't say you won't take any money, the way you did last time."

"But it's like getting paid for what I want to do anyway! I'd give anything to have a dog."

"I know. But I'll be gone for nine or ten days, and that's a lot of responsibility. Part of the deal is that I pay you for your time."

"Okay," Allie said with a shrug. "If you insist."

"You talk it over with your parents tonight and let me know. I'll be happy to call them if they'd like me to."

"I'll tell them," Allie promised.

She met up with Dub in the hallway and they headed for Allie's house. She started to tell him what Mr. Henry had said, but he stopped her, saying, "I heard. Hey, if there's a day when you can't watch Hoover for some reason, I'll sub for you." He paused and leered greedily, adding, "And I *do* expect to be paid. Big bucks."

Allie laughed. "Deal."

They were passing by the Luv'n' Pets store window, and stopped again.

"Look, the puppies are all still there," said Allie after counting the furballs on display. She tensed as a familiar shiver crept down her spine and vanished as quickly as it came. "It just happened again," she said.

Dub's face grew alert. "Really? The same feeling you had this morning?" His voice turned thoughtful. "We were right here, too, in the exact same place." After a moment, he said, "It would be kind of creepy, but maybe your ghost died in this very spot. Like in a car accident, or a murder or something."

Allie and Dub both stepped backward, away from "the spot." Then they looked around, as if a mysterious person or other clue might be lurking nearby.

"No yellow police tape," Allie said with a nervous laugh. "No bloodstains on the sidewalk. Besides, I had the same feeling today in school, not just here."

"Stay tuned for further developments in the Allie Nichols Ghost Case," Dub intoned in the deep, mellow voice of a TV news announcer.

Allie said goodbye to the puppies, and she and Dub walked the rest of the way to her house. Michael was zooming around the driveway on his Big Wheel.

"Hi, Mike," Allie called. "Guess you're feeling better, huh?"

Instead of answering, Michael charged full-speed toward her, making a roaring engine sound.

"I would say the answer to that is yes," said Dub with a grin.

Michael screeched to a halt in front of them. "Watch this!"

He pedaled as hard as he could in the opposite direction, toward the garage. When it appeared that he was going to run straight into the closed garage door, Allie shrieked, "Mike! Stop!"

Michael wrenched his handlebars to the right, and the Big Wheel skidded around in a half-circle. Michael beamed at them, his cheeks pink from exertion and excitement.

"Cool move, Mike!" said Dub.

At the same time, Allie said, "You nearly gave me a heart attack!"

"Watch! I'll do it again!" Michael shouted.

"No, Mike!" She put her hands over her eyes. "I can't look." She and Dub went into the kitchen, where Mrs. Nichols was putting away groceries.

"Hi, Mom."

"Hi, Allie. Hi, Dub."

"Hi, Mrs. Nichols. I'm no doctor, but I'd say Michael's feeling better."

Allie's mother laughed. "It's the oddest thing. He was a mess this morning—stuffy nose, swollen eyes, sneezing, the works. We got in the car, and by the time we got to the doctor's office, he was perfectly fine. Dr. Waheed said he certainly didn't seem sick. We're supposed to watch him for signs of allergies and begin his medicine if he seems to need it. The whole thing was kind of embarrassing, really, after I begged the secretary to squeeze us in."

"Did you have a chance to get the stuff for the dog treats?" Allie asked.

"I got everything on the list." Mrs. Nichols pointed to some items on the countertop. "I had to go to three different places to find it all."

Dub looked through the pile of bags, jars, and boxes and read the labels out loud. "Defatted soy flour, buckwheat groats, brewer's yeast, ground bone meal, bean curd, wheat germ . . . This stuff sounds nasty, Al. I thought you said these cookies are supposed to be *good* for dogs?"

"They are," Allie answered indignantly. "Those things are all super-healthy."

"Low-calorie, too, you said?"

Allie nodded. "For dogs like Hoover, who need to lose weight."

"Oh, *now* I get it," said Dub. "They lose weight because they never eat more than one!"

Mrs. Nichols laughed and said, "I have to admit I had the same thought when I was shopping for the ingredients, Dub."

Allie scowled. "Dub, I thought you came over to help."

"I did," Dub said. "I'm trying to help poor Hoover."

Mrs. Nichols covered her mouth and quickly left the room, but Allie knew she was smiling behind her hand.

Allie glared at Dub. "Can we get started now?"

Making the dog treats was a lot like baking cookies. Allie and Dub mixed the dough, rolled it out, and used the bone-shaped cookie cutter. When the first batch came out of the oven and had cooled, Allie took one of the lumpy, brown bone shapes for herself and handed one to Dub.

"You're kidding, right?" Dub asked wide-eyed.

"We've got to at least *try* them."

Dub sniffed the bone a few times. "I promise you, Allie, if this thing kills me, my ghost will definitely come back to haunt you."

"Except I'll be dead, too. So there," said Allie. "Here goes." She took a crunchy bite of the cookie and began to chew.

Dub watched for a second, then did the same.

"Yuck!" cried Allie, reaching for a paper towel. She spat the rest of the cookie into it.

"Double yuck!" Dub grabbed for a paper towel of his own. He fell to the floor, shaking all over, his tongue hanging out, eyes rolling back in their sockets. Then he stiffened, looked up at Allie, and whispered, "Am I dead?"

"Unfortunately not," said Allie breezily, stepping over him to begin rolling out another batch of dough. "If you think about it, it's actually a good sign that we think they taste bad."

"How do you figure?" asked Dub, reaching for the edge of the countertop to pull himself to his feet.

"Dogs *like* disgusting things," Allie answered. "You wouldn't believe the gross stuff Hoover tries to eat when I take her for walks. Like, one time—"

Dub cut her off. "Okay, okay, I get the point. I don't need to hear the gory details."

"Now, don't laugh," Allie warned. "But I was thinking that if Hoover does like these, I—or we, if you want to—could go into business over the summer. I read that three-quarters of the dogs in America are overweight."

Dub had looked dubious when Allie began, but she could see he was already warming to the idea. "Maybe we could get Luv'n' Pets to sell them," he said. "You know James, the kid who lives next door to me? He works there part-time."

"Do you really think it will work?" asked Allie.

"We'll make millions!"

They smiled at each other for a minute, imagining it. Then Allie said, "Before we get carried away, let's see how Hoover reacts tomorrow. Maybe she'll hate them more than we did."

When three batches had come out of the oven and there was just a little dough left, they cut it in strips and made letters: two *H*'s for Hoover and Mr. Henry, an *A* for Allie, and a *D* for Dub, which came out looking more like an *O* after it was baked.

The letters reminded Allie of L.J. "You know what he said to me today?" she asked.

Dub didn't ask, Who? He knew she was talking about L.J. That was one of the many great things about Dub, in Allie's opinion. His brain and hers seemed to be on the same wavelength. If only he could see ghosts, too . . .

Allie didn't really understand *why* she was able to see ghosts. Or why Michael could, too, when neither of their parents seemed to have the same ability. Or the same curse, depending on how you looked at it. Most of the time, Allie chose to see being a ghost magnet as cool and exciting . . . except when it was absolutely terrifying.

She'd always been aware that there was more to most people than could be seen at a glance. She sometimes wondered if her interest in what lay beneath the surface was the reason ghosts were drawn to her. But Dub was a lot like her in that respect, and he'd never been contacted by a ghost. Why Allie had was one of life's many mysteries.

"So what did L.J. say to you?" Dub asked. He sounded a little impatient, as if he'd asked the question before, while Allie had been preoccupied.

"He said, 'I don't need you or anybody else for a baby-sitter, so just back off.' "

Dub whistled under his breath. "Nice."

"I didn't want to agree with Karen," Allie said, "but he gives me the creeps."

"That makes three of us," said Dub. "Do you think he'll come back tomorrow?"

"I hope not."

Three

When Allie arrived at her classroom the next morning, her wish seemed to have come true. There was no sign of L.J. Most of the other kids were already there, gathered around Hoover, who was lying on the floor on her back, having her belly and throat and ears rubbed. Her eyes were closed and she was grinning in ecstasy. Allie dropped to her knees next to Brad Lewis and joined in, leaning down to give Hoover a kiss on the end of her soft black nose.

"Don't look now, Al," Dub said quietly, with a nod toward the door, "but he's back."

Allie did look. L.J. and a man with the same dark hair were standing together just inside the room. Watching them, Allie decided that *together* wasn't exactly the right word. Even though they stood quite near each other, they appeared to be miles apart. L.J. stood with his back to the man. His arms were folded tightly across his chest, and he glared stonily at a spot on the floor. The man, who Allie figured had to be his father, gazed around the room. He ignored the kids, but when he saw Hoover he looked at the dog for a long time before giving a short nod of what might have been approval.

Allie smiled to herself, thinking, *No one can resist Hoover.*

Then Mr. Cutler, if that was who he was, glanced at Mr. Henry. Giving L.J. a shove, he said, "You won't have no more trouble with him." Before Mr. Henry had a chance to answer, Mr. Cutler turned on his heel and left.

L.J., pushed off balance, stumbled a few steps farther into the room. He stood there, motionless, scowling at the floor.

The room was quiet for a moment. The kids looked uneasily from L.J. to Mr. Henry and back again. The bell that signaled the beginning of school broke the silence. All the students except L.J. went to their desks and sat down.

"L.J.," Mr. Henry said gently, "you may take the seat you had yesterday."

Without acknowledging Mr. Henry, L.J. slid into his chair and assumed the same slouched posture as he had the day before. Allie sneaked a peek at him from the corner of her eye and immediately looked away. His face was so twisted up with anger—or hatred, or *something*, she didn't know what—that it frightened her.

At the same time, a part of her felt sorry for him. She couldn't imagine how she would feel if her father acted as L.J.'s had. But her father would never do anything like that.

Before she knew what she was doing, she whispered, "Hi, L.J."

L.J. didn't respond. Hostility flowed from him in waves she thought she could actually sense against her arm and the side of her face. She felt like a fool.

That's it, she thought. *I'm never speaking to you again.*

She tried to pay attention to what Mr. Henry was saying.

"Well, guys, I can hardly believe it, but this is it. The end of the year."

Allie couldn't help being sad about that. Her feelings must have shown on her face, because when she looked at L.J., he was grinning at her mockingly. She turned away, furious. At that moment, she was glad it was the last day of school so she wouldn't have to sit next to him, wouldn't have to *see* him, all summer.

Mr. Henry suggested that while they cleaned out their desks, they could reminisce about their favorite moments during the year. With an already empty desk and no memories to share, L.J. sat staring at his desktop. Allie had to wonder once more what he was doing at school, but she was determined not to allow him to ruin the last day for her.

"Remember when Hoover came on our field trip to the apple farm and we found her in the barn rolling in cow manure?" Dub was saying.

The class groaned.

"On the way there you were all fighting over who got to sit with her on the bus," Mr. Henry said. "But on the way back, as I recall, she was all mine."

Everybody laughed.

"The coolest thing was on the trip to Fossil Glen, when she dug up Lucy Stiles's dead body," Joey said in his usual loud, booming voice.

A murmur went through the class as the kids remembered that day, and Allie shivered despite herself. She had been the only person present when Hoover had discovered Lucy's remains buried in the cliffside. Then Lucy's killer had shown up, and Hoover had run back to find Mr. Henry and the rest of the class, leaving Allie alone, face-to-face with a murderer. Lucy's ghost had been there, too, fortunately for Allie.

"I don't know if *cool* is the right word," said Julie Horwitz. "But if we're talking about things we'll never forget, that's definitely one of them."

"That's for sure," said Pam Wright. The rest of the kids nodded in agreement.

Allie couldn't help noticing that suddenly L.J. seemed to be listening to what was going on. She supposed talk of finding a dead body might get anyone's attention, even his.

Then, to her surprise, L.J. spoke. Without raising his hand, he said, "You ever breed her?"

He was speaking to Mr. Henry, who appeared confused by the question. Allie felt confused for a moment, also, until she figured out that L.J. had to be asking about Hoover. She was thinking that it was a very peculiar question to ask out of the blue, when a tingle passed over the back of her neck. At the same time, she heard inside her head the desperate crying she'd followed in her nightmare. Even odder, she smelled something awful—something "poopy," to use Michael's word. She looked around to see if any of the other kids were sniffing or wrinkling their noses or giggling, but nobody else seemed to have noticed the odor.

If this was a message from her ghost, she didn't have any idea what it meant. She wanted to focus on it and see if she could learn more, but at the same time she was interested in L.J.'s question and wanted to hear Mr. Henry's answer.

"No," Mr. Henry was saying. "Hoover's a little young for that. She's not even two yet."

L.J. shrugged and said, "Looks old enough."

Mr. Henry shook his finger toward Hoover and said sternly, "No boyfriends for you yet, young lady. No dates for a long, long time."

The kids laughed, except for L.J.

Mr. Henry went on. "I was told it's healthier for the mother if she's at least three when she has her first litter. It's better for the puppies, too, I understand."

It was impossible to tell from L.J.'s impassive expression what he thought about that.

Joey said, "Hoover still acts like a puppy herself half the time."

"You're right about that," said Mr. Henry. He looked toward Hoover and his fond smile turned to a puzzled frown. "What's the matter, girl?"

Hoover was crouched beneath Mr. Henry's desk, whining and rubbing her paws back and forth over her ears.

"She didn't like that talk about having puppies," Pam said with a laugh.

Some other kids laughed, too, and Allie had to agree that it seemed as if Hoover was trying to shut out something she didn't want to hear. But the way she was hiding under the desk made Allie think she'd been spooked. As Allie had learned, Hoover was definitely aware of the presence of ghosts. Was that the cause of her odd behavior?

"My dog does that when he needs his ear medicine," Brad said.

"Maybe that's it," Mr. Henry said.

Hoover looked up then, as if to ask, *Why is everyone staring at me?* The shivery feeling Allie had had was gone, and so was the peculiar odor. The crying sound inside her head had faded, too.

Hoover stood up as if nothing unusual had happened and went over to sniff the table where all the party food and drinks were waiting.

"Well," said Mr. Henry, "it appears that Hoover has decided it's party time!"

Allie tried to push aside the questions in her head and enjoy the party. During the punch and cake and cookies, Mr. Henry handed out blank journals, his end-of-the-year gifts to them all. "So you'll keep up the habit of writing," he explained.

A few of the kids besides Allie had presents for Mr. Henry. Allie was pleased when he took off Hoover's old collar and replaced it with her handmade one, exclaiming over the clever idea of adding Hoover's name and phone number.

She and Dub watched anxiously as Hoover sniffed the bag holding their homemade treats. Mr. Henry gave her one. Hoover chewed it quickly, wagged her tail, and barked.

"She wants another one!" said Joey.

Dub and Allie gave each other the "thumbs-up" sign.

"It's okay, Mr. Henry," said Allie. "They're low-calorie."

Hoover ate a couple more cookies while the kids polished off the food on the table and Mr. Henry opened the rest of his gifts. Then he gave out report cards and, all of a sudden, sixth grade was over.

The kids who rode buses were dismissed first. Allie wasn't the least bit sorry to see Karen Laver leave right after them. L.J., she noticed, slipped out the instant the bell rang. But most of the walkers, Allie and Dub included, hung around, reluctant to leave. Finally, they were the only two kids left.

"Did you have a chance to talk to your parents about taking care of Hoover, Allie?" Mr. Henry asked.

Allie nodded. "They said it was fine."

"And I can help if Allie needs it," added Dub.

"So I guess we're all set, aren't we, girl?" Allie bent down to pat Hoover's smooth, soft ears.

"Great!" said Mr. Henry. "I'd like to leave tomorrow, so I'll have a chance to get organized out there. But I could wait until Sunday."

"Tomorrow's fine with me," said Allie.

"Terrific. I'll give Hoover her breakfast before I go. Later, you can take her for a walk, and go back at dinnertime. Well, I don't have to tell you. Just follow the same routine as before."

"Okay."

Then Mr. Henry said, "I'm glad you both stayed. I have another favor to ask."

"Shoot," said Dub.

"I've been thinking about L.J., and how hard it must have been for him to move to a new place right at the end of the year. He's got the whole summer ahead of him, and he didn't have a chance to get to know anybody or make any friends."

He didn't try very hard, Allie thought. She had a bad feeling about what might be coming next and, sure enough, it did.

"I was hoping you two might make an effort to include him in some of your summer activities. Maybe give him a call if you're going to do something, or stop by to say hi if you're out riding your bikes. What do you think?"

There was a moment's silence while Allie and Dub looked at each other.

"I don't think L.J. likes me very much, Mr. Henry," Allie said at last. *And I certainly don't like him,* she added to herself.

Mr. Henry nodded. "I can see how you'd think that, Allie," he said. "But I doubt it was you he didn't like."

"He didn't seem too happy about being here," Dub said.

Mr. Henry nodded in agreement. "There could be a lot of reasons for that. We don't really know L.J."

Allie felt that she knew enough. She didn't want to disappoint Mr. Henry, but she didn't want to spend any more time with L. J. Cutler, either.

"I keep thinking about something you said, Allie, when you decided to interview Mrs. Hobbs for your Elders Day project," Mr. Henry continued.

"Something *I* said?" Allie echoed.

Mr. Henry nodded. "The class thought you were crazy. They all thought Mrs. Hobbs was weird and scary because of the way she looks."

Allie smiled. Now that she'd gotten to know Mrs. Hobbs, she hardly noticed the cafeteria lady's appearance, which had caused the students, including Allie, to call her the Snapping Turtle.

Mr. Henry continued. "You said, 'We've all known Mrs. Hobbs since kindergarten, but we don't really *know* her.' I was so proud of you that day. You reminded all of us that our first impressions of people don't always tell the whole story."

Great. It was her own big mouth that had gotten her into this. How could she say now that she wouldn't give L.J. another chance?

She looked at Dub. "Okay," they both said, at almost the same instant. "We'll do it."

Mr. Henry beamed at them. "I was thinking last night about who I could ask to do this, and out of all the kids in the class, I came up with you two." He looked serious for a moment. "It might not work out, I understand that. But I appreciate that you're willing to give it a try."

Allie forced herself to smile back at him. She told herself that he was right, that *she* had been right when she said there was more to people than first met the eye.

But she wasn't the least bit convinced this was true of L. J. Cutler.

Four

The entire summer lay before them, but Allie and Dub weren't experiencing the lighthearted, happy feeling they ordinarily had on the last day of school. As they walked home, they discussed their promise to Mr. Henry.

"We were goners the second he brought up Mrs. Hobbs," Dub said.

Allie nodded gloomily. From her pocket she took the piece of paper on which Mr. Henry had written L.J.'s address and phone number. "He lives on Dundee Road," she read. "I've never even heard of it."

"I think it's way out past the old bean packing plant," Dub said.

"There's nothing out there," Allie said.

"Not much," Dub agreed. "There's a place we go every year to cut our own Christmas tree. But that's about it."

"I say we go see him tomorrow," Allie declared. "We'll show up, he'll tell us to get lost, and that will be it. We can tell Mr. Henry we tried."

"Excellent idea," said Dub. "Then we can get on with our plan for making a million dollars selling dog treats."

They were approaching Luv'n' Pets. "You want to stop in and see what they think of our idea?" Allie asked.

"Sure, why not?" answered Dub.

"Look," Allie said, pointing excitedly toward the window, where six furballs now lay curled together on the newspapers. "One of them is gone!" She imagined the scene: the happy puppy in its new home, being cuddled by its loving owner, a girl Allie's own age. *If only Michael weren't allergic,* she wished for what had to be the thousandth time.

When they got inside, Dub went up to the red-haired woman behind the counter, whose nametag said ENID, and asked, "Is James here?"

"Tomorrow," Enid answered. "He works all day on Saturdays."

"Oh," said Dub.

Allie, unable to help herself, said, "I see somebody bought one of the puppies."

Enid hesitated for a moment before answering. "That's right."

"Did a family buy it? People with kids?"

Enid didn't answer but asked pointedly, "Is there something I can help you with?"

Allie was still caught up in her fantasy of the puppy and its new owner. "Was it somebody from around here?"

Enid frowned. "That's none of your business. It's private information."

"Oh," said Allie, stung by the woman's sharp tone. "I wasn't trying to be nosy. I was just wondering if I might see the puppy in the neighborhood, you know, out for a walk or something, that's all. It was so cute . . ." Her voice trailed off under Enid's disapproving glare.

Dub jumped in then, much to Allie's relief. "Uh, you're the owner of the store, right?"

Enid nodded. "I bought it six months ago. Why?"

"Well, the reason we stopped in," Dub began, "is that we have developed a wonderful new pet product, and we wanted to give Luv'n' Pets the opportunity to carry it."

Enid eyed him with suspicion. Lots of kids would have faded under that steely gaze, but Dub just smiled and waited. Allie was enjoying his performance.

"What exactly is this 'wonderful product'?" Enid asked at last.

Allie heard the sarcastic edge to the question, but Dub kept on talking as if he and Enid were old buddies.

"Did you know that three-quarters of American dogs are overweight?" Dub asked. Without waiting for Enid to answer, he went on. "I know, it's shocking, isn't it? So we have developed a low-calorie dog treat made from one hundred percent natural, healthy ingredients, *and—*" Here Dub paused dramatically, smiling broadly at Enid, who stared back stone-faced. "The best part is, people can still indulge their pets without making them fat!"

Enid didn't say anything, but Allie thought she looked interested. At least she hadn't told them to leave. Allie knew she should pitch in and give Dub a little help, but she was distracted by a pathetic whimpering in her head. "Dogs really love them," she said, trying to sound enthusiastic.

There was a long silence, during which Allie began to wonder if Enid had pushed a secret buzzer under the counter and was waiting for the police to arrive and drag them away. She was about to say, "Come on, Dub, let's go," when Enid spoke in a loud, nasal voice.

"You gotta package the stuff in something appealing. Something interesting-looking. And you've got to have a label with a complete list of ingredients."

"No problem," said Dub.

"Bring some in. I'll look them over, maybe test them out on some of the stock. *If* I decide to carry them, you don't get any money up front, understand? You'll get paid only when they sell."

She turned away and began clicking on a computer.

Allie looked at Dub and raised her eyebrows. Enid kept on typing, ignoring them. Finally Dub said cheerily, "Okay, then, we'll see you soon with the first delivery."

Enid didn't answer, so Dub and Allie exchanged a glance and started to leave. When they were almost out the door, Enid spoke again. "I assume, of course, that these things are made under the strictest sanitary conditions."

"Oh, absolutely," Allie said. "The kitchen at our headquarters is immaculate."

She felt herself starting to smile, and Dub pushed her quickly out of the shop. Once outside, she collapsed in a fit of giggles.

"Oh, that's real businesslike, Al," Dub said. "Are you trying to blow the whole deal?"

"Sorry," Allie said, gasping, "but she was too much!" She imitated Enid's loud, grating voice.

Dub began to grin, too. "But we're in!" he said. "She's going to carry them."

Allie nearly choked. "Dub! You actually want to do business with her?"

"Why not? We don't have to be her best friend. All we need is some space on her shelf. Our treats will sell themselves! We'll make millions, remember?"

Allie looked at him dubiously.

"Well, hundreds, anyway," he amended sheepishly.

Allie laughed.

"Possibly thousands. You'll see."

Allie didn't have the heart to burst his bubble. She supposed it couldn't hurt to make another batch of dog treats and bring them to the store. But there was something creepy about that place, something other than Enid.

"Dub," she said, "the whole time we were in there, I heard dogs whimpering."

"So?" said Dub, looking puzzled. "It *is* a pet store. And there *were* six puppies there."

"I know," said Allie. "But they were all asleep."

"You mean—?"

"Yeah. This was the ghost again."

Five

Allie woke from the very same horrible dream she'd had two nights before. As she lay on her back, trying to calm herself, Michael came into her room and climbed under the blanket with her, sniffling miserably. He curled up beside her and let out a sneeze that shook the bed.

"Mike!" Allie cried, sitting up and turning on the light. When she saw his red, swollen face, she reached over to hug him. "What's the matter, big guy?"

"It was awful," Michael said, his lower lip trembling as he struggled not to cry.

"What was awful, Mikey?" she asked, continuing to hold his small, warm body.

"My dream," he said, before exploding with another sneeze.

An uneasy feeling swept through Allie. "You had a scary dream?" she asked.

She felt him nod against her chest.

"What happened in your dream?" she asked, afraid that she already knew.

"I was in a place, a bad place, and it was lost," Michael said. "And I was looking for it, but I was lost, too, and I could hear it, but I couldn't find it." He took a hiccuping breath and continued. "And I kept getting more lost, and I *couldn't find it*, Allie, I *couldn't*!" he finished with a shuddering sob.

Allie let him cry for a minute. When he had settled down, she whispered, "What was it you were looking for, Mike? Could you tell?"

"I couldn't see it," he said shakily. "I could only hear it."

So it was true. She and Mike were dreaming the same dream. She had discovered a couple of weeks before that Mike could see ghosts, too. And now this. Allie needed to think, but first she had to comfort Michael. She hugged him fiercely, wanting to protect him from all scary, hurtful things.

"Ow, Allie! You're squishing me!"

"Oops, sorry, Mike. You want to know something weird?"

"Yeah."

"Promise to keep it a secret?" Allie knew Michael loved secrets.

"Yeah!" He sat up, looking eager.

"I had the exact same dream."

Michael's eyes grew big. "Really?"

"Yes. And I had it once before, too. Did you?"

Michael looked thoughtful for a moment, as if he were trying to remember something. Then he nodded.

"Was it two nights ago?" Allie asked.

Michael shrugged and shook his head. "I don't know."

"Was somebody crying in your dream?"

Michael nodded.

"What did it sound like?"

Michael made a low whimpering sound, very much like the one Allie had heard both in her dream and afterward in her head.

"That's what I heard, too," said Allie. "What did you think it was?"

Michael's expression grew solemn. "I don't know," he said. "But it was sad."

Allie felt sad, too—for Michael, who had been badly frightened, and for whoever was trying so desperately to tell them something. "Do you want to stay in here with me tonight?" she asked.

Michael nodded sleepily.

"Okay, here." Allie reached over to the night table and grabbed a tissue from the box. "Blow."

Michael gave a noisy honk on the tissue, but he still sounded stuffy when he whispered good night to her. She could hear him sniffling and breathing loudly through his mouth as he fell into a restless slumber beside her.

There was no way Allie could go to sleep. She lay awake, making a mental list of everything she knew so far about this new ghost.

One: It was sad.

Two: While the other two ghosts she'd encountered had communicated in words, sometimes even in writing, this one had not, at least not so far.

Three: This ghost had communicated through dreams, sounds, and, she was pretty sure, that odd, yucky smell.

Beginning with the weird feelings she'd gotten at school, she tried to recall everything that had been going on whenever she'd felt the presence of the ghost.

The first time had been on Thursday, right after L.J.'s arrival, when Mr. Henry had told L.J. to sit beside Allie and he had made his rude remark. Allie had been angry with L.J., and a little frightened by him.

The next communication at school had taken place on the last day. All the kids had been at their desks, talking about the past year's events. L.J., she remembered, had acted thoroughly bored until the subject of Hoover came up, when he had begun talking to Mr. Henry about Hoover having puppies. Hoover, Allie recalled with a smile, hadn't liked that idea. But her smile faded as she remembered Hoover's odd behavior, behavior that had reminded her that Hoover, as well as Michael, could sense the presence of ghosts.

Then Allie thought about the three times she'd had ghostly feelings at the pet shop. Twice when she and Dub were outside watching the new puppies in the window, and then again when they were inside talking to Enid.

Two of the incidents featured L.J. Four of them involved dogs or puppies. The dreams had contained the same whimpering that Allie had heard both at the pet shop and at school. All the communications had come from a ghost who wouldn't talk to her.

Allie ran these facts over and over through her tired brain. Then, lying in the dark beside Michael, she took a sharp breath. The pieces of the puzzle fell together and she *knew*.

The ghost wasn't talking because it couldn't.

It was trying to reach her through sounds and smells because those were all it had.

Michael had awakened with allergy attacks both times he had had the scary dream.

Michael was allergic to dogs.

This ghost was a dog.

It seemed so obvious all of a sudden that Allie felt stupid for not figuring it out earlier. At the same time, it struck her as almost silly—a *ghost dog*? Who could blame her for not thinking of *that*? She almost laughed, until she remembered the sound of those pleading cries.

Okay, so her ghost was a dog. And it needed her help.

Six

Allie awoke next to Michael. It was the first day of summer vacation, the first day of doggy-sitting for Hoover, and the first day she knew that her latest ghost was a dog. She couldn't wait to talk to Dub.

During her previous adventures with ghosts, she and Dub had used the computer to find facts about the spirit world. They had learned that a ghost returned to the world of the living because it had a mission to fulfill. A spirit might have to right a wrong or an injustice, reveal important information, exact revenge, or accomplish something else that would allow it to rest in peace.

What pressing business could cause a dog to have a restless spirit? She *had* to talk to Dub.

"Mike," she said softly. "Come on, get up."

Michael wriggled around a bit, then opened his eyes sleepily. Allie could see that the allergic reaction to his dream encounter with the ghost dog hadn't worn off completely yet. She handed him another tissue.

"You okay?" she asked.

Michael nodded, wiping his nose.

"Remember, the dream is our secret, okay?"

Michael nodded again.

Allie felt guilty about making Michael join her in a secret from their parents. But she had never figured out how to explain to them that she and Michael were both ghost magnets.

Her mother and father were basically great. They were nice and funny and always tried to understand her, but they tended to worry about her "overactive imagination." Once she'd heard them talking in worried voices about having her see a psychiatrist. She didn't even want to imagine trying to tell a shrink she saw ghosts. It was one of those things that grownups, parents and probably doctors in particular, just wouldn't get.

Allie didn't want her mother and father to be concerned about her now, not when summer vacation had just begun. She needed as much freedom as possible to solve the mystery of this latest ghost.

It was easier all around to let them think everything was fine. Which it was, really, she told herself. Except for the matter of poor Michael having an allergy attack every time the ghost showed up.

But before anything else, she needed to call Dub. She let him grumble a little about being awakened so early on the first morning of vacation. Then she hit him with the news. She told him how she had figured it out, taking him step by step through her reasoning process.

"Wow!" he said, immediately sounding fully awake. "Weird. But it makes sense, I guess." He added thoughtfully, "As much sense as anything else about ghosts."

"I thought my other two ghosts were frustrating," Allie said ruefully. "I didn't realize until now how helpful it was that they could *speak*."

"Don't worry, we'll figure it out," said Dub. "But first things first. You have to walk Hoover. And we said we were going to L.J.'s today to get that over with. I was thinking we could kill two birds with one stone. We could walk to L.J.'s with Hoover on the leash. Then we'll have the rest of the day to try to crack the case."

Allie loved when Dub used expressions such as "crack the case." It made what they were doing sound so official. Even better was the confidence with which he said *they* would figure it out.

"Great idea," she said. "Except isn't it kind of far to walk?"

"Not really," said Dub. "It's probably only a mile and a half, maybe two miles each way."

"We can take some food and drinks in our backpacks," said Allie, warming to the idea. "And some water for Hoover."

"It'll be good exercise for her. Part of her healthy new lifestyle. Don't forget to pack lots of low-cal treats," Dub added slyly.

"When will you be here?" Allie asked.

"Half an hour."

"Perfect."

Allie went downstairs and joined her mother and Michael at the kitchen table.

"Hi, Mom."

"Morning, sweetie."

"Did Mike tell you he got into bed with me last night?"

"Yes. He said he had a bad dream, but he won't tell me what it was about. He says it's a secret."

Allie looked at Michael and he gave her a conspiratorial smile. She didn't want to start talking about the dream. Michael loved the idea of secrets, but he wasn't very good at keeping them. He'd already said more than Allie would have liked. Quickly, she held her finger to her lips, then turned back to her mother.

"Well, he was really stuffed up again. Don't you think he should start taking his allergy medicine? I'll be seeing Hoover a couple times every day for the next week or so, and I'll probably have dog cooties or whatever you call them all over me."

Mrs. Nichols looked at Michael, who did appear miserable. "You know, I think you're right, Allie."

She got up from the table and went to the phone. Allie heard her leaving a message on Dr. Waheed's answering machine, saying that she was starting Michael on the pills the doctor had prescribed.

Good, Allie thought. Even if the effect of the dream dog wore off later in the day, there was no telling when its ghost might appear to her or to Michael again. This way, Michael would be protected, at least from sniffles and red eyes.

"Michael and your dad are going fishing today," Mrs. Nichols said, returning to the table. "Do you want to go with them? I'm sure they'd wait until you got back from Mr. Henry's house."

"Well, I would, but Dub and I talked about taking Hoover for kind of a major walk. The vet told Mr. Henry she needs to lose weight, so we thought it would help. We're going to pack a lunch and everything. Is that okay?"

"Where are you going?" her mother asked.

"Over to this kid L.J.'s house. He showed up at school for the last two days, and Mr. Henry asked us if we'd be nice to him this summer 'cause he didn't have time to make any friends."

"That was thoughtful of Mr. Henry," said Mrs. Nichols. "And you and Dub, too."

"Well, Dub and I don't really want to do it," Allie confessed.

Her mother looked surprised. "Why not?"

"We didn't like L.J. too much."

"Really?" Mrs. Nichols asked. "Why is that?"

"We think there's something creepy about him," Allie said.

Her mother looked at her and scolded gently, "Allie, you're not letting your imagination run away with you again, are you? After all, you've only seen the boy at school—what?—twice? How could you know what he's like?"

"That's what Mr. Henry said," Allie admitted with a sigh. She wanted to add, *But sometimes even a cool teacher like Mr. Henry can be kind of clueless.* She didn't, though. And she certainly didn't want her mother to get started on her "runaway imagination" again. Instead she said, "We promised Mr. Henry we'd give him a chance, so that's what we're doing."

"Well, I think that's very nice."

Easy for you to say, Allie thought. *You've never met L.J.*

Seven

Soon Allie and Dub were letting themselves in through the door of Mr. Henry's kitchen. "Hoover?" Allie called. "We're here, girl. Ready for food and a walk?"

When the dog's bowl was empty, Allie took the leash from its place in the closet. Hoover began prancing around the room with excitement, her tail wagging like a furry, golden flag.

"I'd say she's ready," declared Dub.

"Let's go."

They walked slowly, letting Hoover stop to sniff wherever she pleased. Observing this behavior, Allie said, "Maybe if we watch Hoover carefully, we'll learn something that will help. Look at her nose go. She can probably tell which dogs already passed by that signpost this morning and when."

"You said you and Michael were smelling something disgusting, right?"

Allie wrinkled her nose. "Yeah, it was gross."

Watching Hoover happily slurping water from a muddy puddle, Dub said, "Gross to you. To a dog it might be delectable."

"True," Allie said. "But maybe trying to think like a dog isn't such a great idea. Probably we should try to imagine the kind of thing that might happen to a dog to make it into a restless ghost."

Dub looked thoughtful. "Well, there's the obvious car accident. A hit-and-run driver."

"And remember that story that was going around a while ago about some people who got mad at their neighbors' dog for barking, so they poisoned it?"

"Yeah," said Dub. "And did you know that some people actually raise dogs for fighting? They make bets on which dog will win, and sometimes one dog kills the other one."

Allie shuddered. "That is totally sick. Actually, this whole conversation is a real bummer."

"You started it." They walked in silence for a while before Dub added, "The only other thing I can think of is that dogs sometimes get used for scientific experiments."

"Gee, there's another cheerful thought," Allie said bleakly. "But, cheerful or not, we have to get used to thinking about this stuff. Because one thing we've learned is that ghosts are unhappy for a reason."

Soon they were approaching the old bean packing plant. It gave Allie the willies. The gray paint was peeling badly, giving the walls what she thought of as a scabby, unhealthy appearance. Most of the windows had been broken and lay in sharp, glittering shards on the ground. A sheet of metal roofing had torn loose and was flapping erratically in the wind with a hollow clang. The abandoned hulk of a building looked cold in contrast to the sunny glare of the empty parking lot, and an odd odor of decay drifted from it.

Allie walked faster, feeling silly even as she did, and grateful for the company of Dub and Hoover. There were times when, like her parents, she wished her imagination *weren't* quite so vivid.

"Maybe he won't be home," she said, trying to shake the feeling the old plant had given her.

Naturally, Dub knew she was talking about L.J. "I hope he is," he said. "Otherwise, this whole trip is a waste. We'll just have to come back. Or explain to Mr. Henry why we didn't."

"Then we'd better decide what we're going to say when we get there." Allie sighed. "We can't tell him Mr. Henry wanted us to make friends with the poor little new kid. I can just hear him: 'I told you I don't need no baby-sitter!' "

They continued walking.

"I know," said Allie. "We can say we noticed he seemed to like Hoover, and since we were out walking Hoover, anyway, we decided to stop over." Dub didn't answer right away and Allie added, "Although I'm not exactly sure he *liked* Hoover. It was just that she was the only thing he showed any interest in at all."

"And then we hope he doesn't ask how we found out where he lives," said Dub.

"It's going to be awful however we do it," said Allie. She could feel Dub looking at her closely. "What?" she asked.

"You're not usually so pessimistic," he answered.

Allie shrugged. She wasn't sure why she was letting L.J. bother her so much.

"Relax," Dub said cheerfully. "What can happen? There are three of us and one of him. If he tries anything, Hoover'll lick him, right, girl?"

Hoover grinned a doggy grin, clearly happy to be the focus of their attention, and Allie laughed. "Yeah, Hoover'll go right up and give him a big kiss."

Allie did relax a little, at least until they came to the turn onto Dundee Road. Past a stand of scrubby bushes and a swampy area filled with cattails sat a house, all by itself except for a lopsided barn in the field behind it. A dilapidated mailbox was fixed to a post near the road. The name on it was Keegan, not Cutler, but the number matched the one Mr. Henry had given them.

"This must be it," Allie said, squinting at the house. "I guess they haven't had time to change the name."

The sun was in her eyes, making it difficult to get a good look at the house, but she could see that it wasn't in any better shape than the mailbox. The yard was overgrown and filled with an odd assortment of objects: a stained sink, a rusty wheelbarrow, some cinder blocks, a pink bicycle with tattered streamers hanging from the handles, and a plastic Santa Claus lying on his side near a plastic reindeer. It looked as if someone had used the reindeer for target practice.

The place made Allie very uncomfortable. She turned to Dub, who was looking around curiously. "Creepy, huh?" she said. "Plus, I'm starting to get ghost vibes."

"Oh, great," Dub replied. "What do you think we should do?"

"Go up and knock on the door, I guess."

They climbed up the stairs onto the porch, which was just as cluttered as the yard. There was a stained mattress with stuffing coming out and another with the springs poking through, along with cardboard boxes filled with old magazines, bottles, and cans.

Allie and Dub approached the door, and Allie peered through a rip in the screen to a room that held a couch and a television and not much else. No sign of L.J. She knocked, and she and Dub listened for an answering voice or the sound of footsteps. Hoover began pacing nervously, tugging at the leash and whining softly.

"Shh, Hoovey," whispered Allie. "We'll be going in a minute." She didn't know why she was whispering, exactly, but she kept it up as she said to Dub, "Looks like nobody's here."

Just then a loud screech came from somewhere behind the house, causing Dub and Allie to jump and Hoover to bark in alarm. It took Allie a moment to recognize the sound of a power saw. She and Dub looked at each other and headed in that direction.

When they rounded the back corner of the house, they saw L.J. bent over a piece of plywood held up by two sawhorses. He was carefully making a cut along one edge. Allie had helped her dad on many woodworking projects, and she knew how hard it was to keep a piece of wood from sliding during a long cut if there wasn't a second pair of hands to hold it. Out of habit, she stepped forward to hold the plywood steady.

L.J., immersed in his work and unable to hear over the noise of the saw, jerked upright in surprise. There was a horrible screeching noise as the saw twisted, caught in the wood, and bucked, before L.J. snatched his hand away from the trigger and the saw blade stopped.

For a moment there was quiet. Then L.J. let loose a string of swear words that stunned Allie into speechlessness. Dub, too, seemed struck dumb, and even Hoover stood frozen. They all looked at L.J., who was glaring back, red-faced and breathing hard.

"Sorry," Allie ventured at last. "I was only"—she winced as the full force of L.J.'s stare fell on her—"trying to help."

L.J.'s mouth twisted in a scornful grimace. "You again. Little Miss Fix-it from school. And her boyfriend, looks like."

"Let's go, Dub," Allie said tightly.

"No, you just hold on a second. What are you doing here, anyway?"

"Nothing," said Allie. "We're going."

"I thought I told you to leave me alone."

"Don't worry, we will," Allie answered angrily. "Come on, Dub."

They were about to go when a man came out of the barn and began striding across the field toward them. As he approached, a gust of wind came from behind him and blew his hat off his head and onto the ground. He ignored it and kept coming. Allie could see his face now, and the anger on it frightened her. It was the same man who had pushed L.J. into the classroom at school.

Hoover sniffed the breeze and, to Allie's dismay, let out a long, mournful howl. It was a sound Allie never had heard before from the normally happy dog.

Mr. Cutler strode up to L.J. and snapped, "Shut that dog up!"

Hoover began growling, and Allie knelt beside her to try to quiet her. It was almost as if Hoover sensed danger in the situation and knew she should stop, but couldn't. She sat still, but continued making a low growl deep in her throat.

Mr. Cutler had turned back to L.J., and pointed his thumb toward Allie and Dub. "Who are they?" Without waiting for an answer, he said, "What have I told you about people coming here?"

"I didn't ask them," L.J. said sullenly. "They just showed up."

"Look at the mess you made of that cut," Mr. Cutler said, curling his lip in disgust and pointing to the piece of plywood. A gouge marred the cut where the saw had bucked.

"I startled him," Allie tried to explain. "That's why—"

She felt Dub's elbow poke sharply into her side, signaling her to be quiet.

L.J. stood scowling at the ground, the way he had in school when his father had pushed him.

"How many times have I told you to use these?" the man asked, reaching for a couple of C-shaped clamps and throwing them at L.J.'s feet.

L.J. didn't respond and his father repeated, "I said how many times?"

"Plenty of times," L.J. said at last. He sounded tired.

"That's right," said Mr. Cutler. "Plenty of times. But you think you're so smart you don't need to listen to your father, don't you?"

Although moments before, Allie had been fed up with L.J. herself, she felt a fierce sympathy for him now, seeing him with his father. His *father*! It was difficult for Allie to comprehend. This man was so different from her own funny, gentle dad.

"Don't you?" Mr. Cutler insisted.

L.J. didn't answer. It was a question that didn't have any safe answer, and Allie was glad L.J. didn't try to give one. In the silence that followed, a dog began to bark. Others joined in, forming a chorus. The sound came from the barn, where L.J.'s father had been. Immediately, Hoover barked back.

The barking seemed to enrage Mr. Cutler. He kicked the leg of the sawhorse, and the plywood fell to the ground. "It's always the same," he said furiously, shaking his head at L.J. "You're just like your mother. You never listen."

He started walking toward a gray pickup truck that was parked between the house and the barn. He opened the door, but before he got in, he turned to look back at Allie and Dub. "We don't need you two coming around here. We got work to do. He says he didn't ask you, so why don't you get lost?"

Allie and Dub scrambled to leave, practically tripping over each other and Hoover in their hurry. Allie forced herself to look back just before she rounded the corner of the house. When she did, her eyes locked for a brief moment with L.J.'s. In their darkness, she thought she glimpsed something that might have been sorrow or regret.

Or maybe, she told herself as she ran across the yard, she had only imagined it.

Eight

Allie and Dub ran down the gravel edge of Dundee Road in silence. When they turned onto the main road, Mr. Cutler drove by, heading in the same direction, back toward town. As he passed, he gazed at them from the open window, his face an expressionless mask.

Only when he was out of sight did Allie speak. "That was so awful, Dub." Her voice came out low, and a little shaky.

Dub, looking troubled, nodded in agreement.

Allie made an effort to slow the beating of her heart and calm herself. She felt almost dizzy from everything that had just happened. Meanwhile, Hoover continued to tug at the leash, looking back the way they had come and whimpering.

"Let's sit down for a minute, okay?" Allie suggested.

They walked about twenty feet away from the road into an overgrown field and sat down under a large maple tree. Allie shrugged off her backpack and took out the little plastic bowl and the bottle of water she'd brought for Hoover, along with the plastic bag filled with some of the dog snacks she and Dub had made.

She poured some water into the bowl, placed it under Hoover's nose, and held out one of the biscuits. Hoover ignored both the water and the treat, pacing restlessly and continuing to whine unhappily.

"I've never seen her refuse food before," Dub said.

"Me neither," said Allie. She reached into her backpack again and took out a package of cheese. "Look, Hoover!" she cajoled, waving a slice under the dog's nose. "People food."

Hoover sniffed once, but to Allie's amazement, paid no further attention. She sat as far away as the leash would allow, looking back toward Dundee Road and making pathetic noises.

Allie and Dub looked at each other in consternation. "What the heck is going on?" Dub asked.

"I don't know," Allie answered. "But, Dub, the whole time we were at that house, my ghost was there. I couldn't exactly concentrate on it with everything else that was going on. I think Hoover felt it, too."

"I think she still does," Dub said, watching Hoover straining at her leash.

Allie nodded. "It got stronger when L.J.'s father came out of the barn. Did you notice how Hoover acted?"

"She got even more agitated when those other dogs started barking," Dub said thoughtfully. "But they were no ghosts—they were real."

"Yeah. So it's hard to tell if it was the ghost that was bothering her, or if she just wanted to go check out the other dogs."

"It sure sounded like a *lot* of other dogs, didn't it?"

Allie nodded.

"What about the ghost? Do you sense it now?" Dub asked.

Allie sat very still for a moment to make sure. "No."

"Then maybe it's something back there that's bugging Hoover," Dub said, gesturing toward the Cutler place. "Hoover"—he pretended to beg—"talk to us, girl. Tell us what's going on."

Hoover raised her muzzle and howled, for all the world as if she were trying to do as Dub had asked. Allie couldn't help laughing nervously, even though it upset her to see Hoover so distressed.

She took a slug of lemonade from the thermos she'd packed, and handed it to Dub. When he'd had a drink, she stood up, saying, "Let's get going.

Maybe if we get farther away from here, Hoover will think about something else."

The tactic seemed to work. Before long, Hoover was trotting happily beside Allie, sniffing each object they passed, pouncing on insects, chasing every leaf and stray bit of trash that blew in the wind.

Allie relaxed a bit on seeing Hoover acting normal again. "It was my fault L.J. messed up the cut he was making," she said.

"You started to say it, too. But I didn't think that was too smart right then, with old man Cutler so ticked off. And what was he so mad about, anyway? One little gouge in the wood, big deal."

"I think it was us being there that really made him mad," Allie replied. "He acted like L.J.'s not allowed to have anybody over."

Dub nodded in agreement. "And when the dogs in the barn barked, that set him off, too."

"Then there was that stuff about how L.J. is just like his mother. It sure didn't sound like a compliment. I wonder where she was?"

"I don't know, but I feel sorry for her, being married to a guy like that," said Dub. He added, "And for L.J., having him for a father."

"Me, too," said Allie. Then she added with frustration, "But it's hard to feel sorry for very long, you know? I mean, why did he have to be so rotten to us? Calling me Little Miss Fix-it—I hate that."

Dub nodded in sympathy.

They were passing the bean packing plant again. The breeze carried the smell of dampness and decay, and lifted that same loose sheet of metal roofing. The sharp clang made Allie jump and quicken her steps. Suddenly, she couldn't wait to be back in the more populated area of town.

As they passed Luv'n' Pets, Allie stopped to look at the puppies. She was surprised to see that only three little furballs lay curled together in the far corner of the display window. Dub peered through the glass and said, "Hey, James is in there. Let's tell him about our business idea."

"Okay," Allie said. "Do you think it's all right to take Hoover in? She's on a leash."

"Al, it's a pet store."

James was alone in the store, cleaning out the cage belonging to a bird Allie recognized as a cockatiel. Allie knew James from seeing him outside when she'd been over at Dub's house.

James smiled at them. "Hey, what's up?"

Allie held tight to the leash as Hoover strained to get closer to the bird. Hoover's nose was going a mile a minute and her tail wagged furiously. The bird fluttered nervously around its cage.

"Sit, Hoover," Allie commanded. To her surprise, Hoover obeyed, and sat as if mesmerized, her eyes fixed on the cockatiel.

Dub told James about their plan to sell dog biscuits at the store. James listened, nodding from time to time as he worked.

"So what do you think?" Dub asked when he'd finished.

"Healthy treats sound like a good idea," James answered carefully.

Allie didn't think this response was very enthusiastic, but Dub seemed satisfied. "Hey, James," she said, "I see three more puppies got sold. Did the same person buy all of them?"

A shadow passed over James's face. After a moment he said brusquely, "No."

Allie waited for James to say more. Instead, he picked up a rag and began wiping the bottom of the cockatiel's cage. His movements were jerky and seemed to Allie to be covering a strong emotion. She looked at Dub, who apparently was as puzzled as she.

"When we were here yesterday, there were six," Dub said. "Enid must have had a busy day."

James didn't comment, but after a few seconds he straightened up, threw the rag to the floor, and said, "Sometimes I really hate working here!"

Allie was taken aback by the vehemence in his voice. She was pretty sure James wasn't referring to cleaning birdcages, but she had no idea what he *was* talking about.

They all stood quietly for a moment, James clenching and unclenching his hands and looking miserable. He appeared to be struggling with himself. Finally, he shook his head and said with a sigh, "Listen, I really need this job. Forget what I just said, okay?"

"Okay," Allie answered, feeling bewildered.

"Because if Enid thinks I told you guys anything," James went on, "I'm history."

"Don't worry about it," Dub said quickly.

"If you want to go into business with her, that's up to you," James said. "Just keep me out of it."

"No problem," Dub said. He looked at Allie and added, "Well, I guess we'd better get going."

She nodded. Then she said softly, "See you, James."

"Yeah," he answered tiredly. "Later."

"Come on, Hoovey," Allie said, giving the leash a gentle tug and heading for the door.

When they reached the sidewalk, Dub turned to Allie and said flatly, "That was weird."

"Very." She was about to say more when Dub stopped dead in his tracks. Following his gaze, she saw that he was looking toward the other side of the street, where a gray pickup truck was maneuvering into a parking spot.

L.J.'s father opened the door of the truck and started across to their side of the street. Allie immediately turned her face away, wanting no chance of another encounter with the man. Dub must have had the same thought, for he looked in the opposite direction, as well.

But they couldn't do anything to hide Hoover. The big dog's appearance was so distinctive that Mr. Cutler probably would notice her, and therefore Dub and Allie, no matter what. Hoover, however, seemed determined not to leave it up to chance. She stood stiffly, totally focused on the figure approaching from the opposite side of the street. When Mr. Cutler stepped onto the curb about twenty feet from Allie and Dub, Hoover lunged toward him so forcefully that she yanked the leash right out of Allie's hand. Then, to Allie's horror, Hoover raced right up to Mr. Cutler, barking frantically.

Not sure what to do, Allie and Dub watched as Hoover danced in circles around L.J.'s father. She feinted forward one moment, teeth bared, then reared back the next, never getting any closer than two feet from the man. All the while, she was making such a racket that other people on the street were stopping to see what was going on.

"Hoover!" Allie shouted. "Come!"

Hoover ignored her. But Mr. Cutler didn't. He raised his head and stared right at her. The menace in his eyes made her shudder. Then she and Dub both sprang into action, running to grab Hoover's leash.

Together, they were able to drag her away, although she never stopped her frantic barking.

"You should learn to control that dog," Mr. Cutler said. As he turned to leave, he added, "Or somebody's gonna do it for you."

Allie and Dub leaned down to soothe Hoover, who was watching Mr. Cutler, and was panting and whining now instead of barking. They watched, too, as Mr. Cutler opened the door of Luv'n' Pets and disappeared inside.

Nine

It had been, in many ways, an upsetting and exhausting morning. After Allie left Dub and took Hoover back to Mr. Henry's house, she went home and fell asleep on the couch in the family room. But her nap was disturbed by dreams.

This time, Allie felt that her ghost was leading her to something it wanted her to see. Somehow, she was able to keep up with the ghost dog's rapid, four-legged pace, so that it was almost as if she were flying over the ground. She was Allie, but she was experiencing the world as a dog!

It was exhilarating to feel so strong and free and fast. She found that she was perceiving the shapes of objects more than their colors, and everything seemed to be lit with the dim haze of sunset. Her sense of hearing was unusually acute, and her sense of smell was incredible. She was moving so quickly that everything was going by in a blur of vivid, intriguing odors, but there was no opportunity to stop and explore them. It was frustrating to ignore the pull of her thrilling canine impulses. All she really wanted to do was race about and follow her nose. But this wasn't a pleasure trip. Allie could feel the sense of urgency from the other dog, leading her onward.

She was being taken through territory that was vaguely familiar, and soon she realized they were following the route that she and Dub had traveled earlier in the day. At one point she recognized the decaying smell that emanated from the abandoned bean packing plant, but it was quickly replaced by other smells, of gravel and grass and dampness and mud and the creatures that lived there. This she recognized, too, as the essence of the swampy area near L.J.'s house.

Then Allie felt that she was back in her other, original dream, running through the maze of walls in the middle of which, somewhere, a dog whimpered. But this time she reached it, with her ghost guide leading her.

Suddenly Allie glimpsed a terrible scene. A dog lay in a small area partitioned off by plywood. A bit of straw was scattered on the bare cement floor, but it was filthy and wet, and the odor Michael had described as "poopy" was unbearable. The dog looked up, its brown eyes dull and almost lifeless.

Nailed to the plywood was a board with a name on it. Each letter was written with a different color crayon in childish block print. The sign read: BELLE.

Slowly surfacing to consciousness, Allie felt burdened by the sadness of this new vision. She lay on the couch contemplating it. Was Belle the ghost dog, showing Allie where she had died? Or was Belle another dog that was still alive and needed help? How frustrating to be lying about safely in her home, when she should be doing something. If only she knew what it was!

Her mother walked into the family room, took one look at Allie, and said, "Honey, do you feel all right?"

"I'm a little tired," Allie said, which was the truth, if not the entire truth. She got up and went to look at herself in the mirror. One side of her face was red and wrinkled from where it had been scrunched against the arm of the couch. That would go away in a few minutes. But there were dark shadows under her eyes, and worry lines creased her forehead. Being a ghost magnet was taking its toll.

Not wanting her mother to become concerned about her health, Allie forced a smile. "What time are we having dinner?" she asked.

"Your dad and Michael will be home shortly. We can eat as soon as they get here. Why, are you hungry?"

"Sort of," Allie said. "But the reason I asked is that I have to go back to Mr. Henry's to feed Hoover. And Dub wants me to go to his house afterward."

This wasn't the whole truth, either. The need for secrecy that went along with seeing ghosts seemed to be making Allie into a habitual liar. But she *was* going to call Dub right away to ask him if she *could* come over. She had to tell him about her dream.

Also, Allie was hoping James would be home. She wanted to ask him what Mr. Cutler had been doing at the pet store.

Ten

Allie was glad to see that Michael showed no signs of allergies at dinner. Since he'd been happily fishing instead of sleeping during the time she'd been having her dream that afternoon, she didn't have to worry about his sharing the disturbing vision she'd had of the dog named Belle.

"It was *this big*, Allie," he was saying, holding his hands way up over his head, about two feet apart. "But I let it go 'cause Dad said it was a mommy and it was full of eggs."

"That's a mighty big perch," Allie said. "The biggest one I ever saw was maybe this long." She held her hands ten inches apart.

"Well, this one was *humongous*, right, Dad?"

"It sure was," Mr. Nichols answered, winking at Allie. "And it's been getting bigger all afternoon."

"The mark of a true fisherman," Mrs. Nichols said with a laugh.

"What is?" Michael asked, looking down at himself as if expecting to see some sort of mark on his chest.

"Throwing back a mommy fish so she can hatch her eggs and make baby fish," Allie answered quickly. "That was a good thing to do, Mike."

Michael nodded proudly. "I know."

"We missed you, Al," said her father.

"I was sorry I couldn't go, Dad," she said. "But Dub and I had to see this kid L.J., and we have to go back to his house tomorrow."

She had a plan, of sorts, for finding out what her dream had been trying to tell her. She and Dub would have to return to the Cutler place, though. She hoped Dub would be game.

"That's nice of you, Allie, but tomorrow is Sunday, remember?" said her mother.

"Oh, right," said Allie. School had just gotten out and she was already getting the days mixed up. Her parents tried to make Sunday a family day. They usually went to church and did something together.

"How about we all go fishing?" Mr. Nichols suggested.

"Okay," said Allie.

"Sounds good to me," said Mrs. Nichols.

"But it's not fair," Michael complained. "Mom and Allie always catch the most fish."

"If you're good, I'll tell you the secret of my success," Allie told him.

"Another secret! Yay!"

Allie frowned at him and held her finger to her lips. Luckily, her parents didn't seem to notice.

"So how was your visit to this boy L.J. today?" asked Mr. Nichols.

Her parents would have a fit if she told them what had happened at the Cutler house that afternoon. Allie would never be allowed to go there again. Not that she *wanted* to go. But the ghost dog had led her in that direction, and if she was going to find any answers, she had to follow every clue.

"Oh, fine," she answered vaguely.

"So you and Dub liked L.J., after all?" asked Mrs. Nichols.

"Well, he seems to need friends," Allie said, silently congratulating herself on coming up with an answer that was, from what she'd seen, true. Not that he was ever likely to make any friends acting the way he did, and with his father making it plain that visitors were not welcome. She didn't plan on being L.J.'s friend, but she did need to return to his house, at least one more time.

"He has some dogs," Allie went on. "So Dub and I

were going to take over some of our homemade dog treats."

"That's nice, sweetie," said her mother. "Were L.J.'s parents home?"

"His father was," Allie answered carefully. "But we never saw his mother. Maybe she'll be there next time." Now that she thought about it, she was curious to see what Mrs. Cutler was like. Probably as unpleasant as her son and husband, Allie told herself.

"So is it okay if Dub and I make another batch of biscuits on Monday morning?"

"Are there any ingredients left?" asked Mrs. Nichols.

Allie nodded.

"Sure. If you clean up after yourselves."

"We will."

"Can I help?" Michael asked.

"There are going to be plenty of chances to help," Allie told him. "Dub and I are going into business."

Her parents wanted to know more, so while Allie cleared the table she told them about the conversation with Enid at Luv'n' Pets. "Dub thinks we're going to make a ton of money," she said, "but I'm not so sure." Actually, she wasn't sure she wanted to get involved with Enid at all, although she couldn't exactly put her finger on the reason.

"I think it's a great idea," said her dad. "Are you ready to turn the kitchen into corporate headquarters, Ann?"

"For a cut of the profits, yes," said Mrs. Nichols. With a smile at Allie, she added, "You and Dub will be hearing from my lawyer."

"Can we watch this now, Mom?" Michael asked eagerly, waving a videotape in the air. Allie caught the title: *Charlotte's Web*.

"In a little while," answered Mrs. Nichols. "First, I want you to have a bath. When you're in your pajamas, we'll make some popcorn and we'll all watch together." To Allie she said, "Sweetie, why don't you feed Hoover and come back and join us? You were with Dub all day."

"I'd like to, Mom, but I can't. I promised." Allie sighed inwardly. It would be nice to have a cozy evening at home with her family, instead of trying to find out more about the unfortunate Belle. She was determined to see this thing through, but she was beginning to dread what she might discover.

Eleven

As Allie approached Mr. Henry's house, she admired the back-yard paradise he'd created for his canine buddy. There was a small door built into the large kitchen door, so Hoover could go out of the house whenever she wanted, into a large, fenced area filled with toys. When Allie showed up on her bike, Hoover was already in the yard, wagging her tail in greeting.

"Hi, Hoovey," said Allie as she let herself into the yard through the gate. "Dinnertime, girl." She knelt down to pet Hoover's silky ears and laughed as the dog covered her face with kisses. "But you knew that, didn't you?"

They went inside, where Allie filled Hoover's food and water dishes and talked to her while she ate. Then they went into the yard for a while, and Allie threw Hoover's favorite toy, a green plastic frog that squeaked, for her to fetch.

After Hoover had had a good romp, Allie gave her a kiss on the nose and promised she'd be back first thing in the morning. Hoover stood by the gate, looking forlorn when Allie climbed onto her bike.

"Please don't look so sad, Hoovey," Allie begged, looking back over her shoulder as she rode away. "I'll see you first thing tomorrow."

Dub was in the driveway shooting baskets when Allie pulled up to his house. "Nice shot," she called as he sunk one. She got off her bike and held out her arms, and he threw her the ball. Her shot hit the rim and bounced off. She caught it, took another try, and missed again. When her third shot went in, Dub grabbed the ball and tossed it expertly under the porch.

Allie told Dub about her latest dream and the poor dog whose name was Belle. They talked about what it might mean and tried to imagine who Belle was, but together they were no more successful than Allie had been on her own.

When they'd worn out the subject of Belle, Dub pointed next door to James's house. He said, "So you want to see if he's home?"

Allie nodded, and they walked across the yard and

knocked on James's door. James answered, looking first surprised to see them, then troubled.

"We just want to ask you something," Allie said quickly.

James stood stiffly in the doorway. "What?" he asked warily.

"Right after we left the store today, a man came in. Do you remember him?"

James looked blank.

"You might have heard a lot of commotion out on the street first. Hoover, the dog that was with me, went kind of crazy on the guy."

James's face cleared. "Oh yeah, I know who you mean."

"What did he want?" Allie asked.

"He wanted to see the owner. I told him Enid wouldn't be in until Monday. He said he'd come back."

"That's it?" said Dub.

James shrugged. "Pretty much. He left a business card."

"What was on the card?" Allie asked.

"I didn't really look at it," James answered. "I left it where Enid would see it." The troubled expression passed over his features again. "Look, why do you guys keep asking me so many questions about the store?"

Allie responded boldly with a question of her own. "Why don't you want to tell us anything?"

"What makes you think there's anything to tell?"

Allie didn't answer, and Dub remained quiet, too. Finally James looked away.

The silence grew.

"Okay, I guess we'd better get going," Allie said. "Thanks, James."

"See ya," said Dub.

James closed the door without answering.

When she was sure they were out of earshot, Allie said, "I don't get it. Something is really bugging him. It's like he wants to talk about it, but—"

"But he doesn't," Dub finished.

"As if he's scared."

"Of what?"

It was another question they couldn't answer. Mentally, Allie added it to her list, a list that was getting longer rather than shorter.

They decided that Allie would get up early on Monday morning to walk and feed Hoover, and that Dub would come to her house afterward, at around ten o'clock, to make dog biscuits to take to L.J. Then they'd go to his house, but without Hoover. They planned to hide and wait, if they had to, until the gray pickup wasn't around. They agreed that if stealth and quiet were required, bringing along the rambunctious and unpredictable dog would be a big mistake.

Twelve

Allie felt almost like a normal person when she went to bed Sunday night. She'd taken care of Hoover and gone fishing with her family, and not one odd, ghostly thing had happened all day long. She slept soundly, with no bad dreams. It was a relief at first, and then became almost a worry. Was she losing her touch?

When Dub came over in the morning to make dog biscuits, she told him of her concern.

"Ghosts are unpredictable," he said, "judging from the ones you've met, anyway. Who knows what a *dog* ghost is likely to do? I wouldn't worry about it."

"I guess you're right," said Allie. "Let's finish this batch and get out to L.J.'s. Maybe we'll learn something."

As soon as the last tray of biscuits had come out of

the oven and they'd had a quick lunch, Allie and Dub rode toward L.J.'s house. They turned onto Dundee Road and immediately stashed their bikes in the bushes. Then they crept along through the tangled, scrubby brush until they could see the Cutler place. There was no sign of the gray pickup. Allie and Dub exchanged glances of relief. Unless Mr. Cutler had parked the truck in the barn, the coast appeared to be clear.

Allie hitched up her backpack. It contained the bag of dog biscuits, which was supposed to be their excuse for coming back. Suddenly, though, their plan didn't seem like such a great idea. What if Mrs. Cutler was the one who was out in the truck, and Mr. Cutler was home, after all? What if L.J. and his mother were both gone, and she and Dub were about to come face-to-face with Mr. Cutler, with no one at all around to protect them? She told herself she was being silly. As if L.J. would protect them. As if he *could* protect them against a man like his father, even if he wanted to.

Allie told herself to stop thinking. It wasn't getting them anywhere. The reality was that, based on a dream journey led by a ghost dog, she and Dub were barging in where they weren't wanted, hoping to get some information, although they had no idea what that information might be. It was a pretty lame plan, but it was all they had. She supposed they might as well get on with it.

"Let's go," she whispered to Dub. "We'll knock, like we did before, and if L.J. doesn't answer, we'll look out back where he was last time. If nobody's around, we can check out the barn."

"Okay," Dub whispered back, then added, "Why are we whispering?"

Allie giggled and Dub grinned. It made her feel braver.

They left the shelter of the bushes and started across the open, swampy ground. Rich odors rose from the wet earth as Allie and Dub squished through the mud, and Allie recognized the smells from her dream, though they were much less intense now than they'd been to her canine nose.

"Man," said Dub, lifting a dripping, muddy sneaker and examining it. "What is this, the Black Lagoon?"

"Keep going," Allie urged him. "If we stop, we might sink in this stuff and never be seen again."

At the Cutlers' yard, the ground was higher and dryer, and they walked among the scattered pieces of junk, trying to scrape some of the mud from their shoes on the browned grass. There was no scream of a saw this time, no sound at all, it seemed. It was almost spookily quiet. Allie was telling herself there was no way anyone was around when a low voice came from the house, nearly scaring her to death.

"I'm about to die laughing watching you two. Just what do you think you're doing?"

Allie gasped and came close to tripping over the pink bicycle, which was still lying in the grass. Dub, too, let out a shout of surprise. Allie looked in the direction the voice had come from, but it took a moment before she saw him.

L.J. was slouched in a shredded lawn chair set back in the shady corner of the porch, with his feet stretched straight out and his arms folded across his chest, just as he had sat next to Allie in school. He was shaking his head and grinning. It wasn't a friendly grin, but a mocking one.

It made Allie furious. "What about *you*, hiding in the dark and spying on people?"

L.J. laughed. "I ain't hiding or spying. I live here, remember? You're the ones sneaking around in the bushes. You come to rob me?" He sneered, lifted his arm, and gestured around the yard. "Help yourselves. Take whatever you want." He sat without moving, watching them, his eyebrows lifted sardonically.

Allie thought she had never met anyone so irritating in all of her life. She was struggling to get control of herself and come up with something to say or do next when Dub said mildly, "Actually, we came to *bring* you something."

Allie took a deep breath and tried to settle down. Dub had the right approach. She couldn't let L.J. bother her. She had to get a grip and be cool, as Dub was doing.

She slipped off her backpack, removed the plastic bag filled with dog biscuits, and held it out toward L.J. "They're dog snacks," she said shortly.

"You came way out here with *dog food*?" L.J. said, sounding both amused and incredulous.

It was all Allie could do not to turn on her heel and stomp away. Hadn't anyone ever told him it was rude to make fun of someone who was giving him something?

"What would I want with *dog food*?"

His jeering tone was really getting on Allie's nerves.

"Oh, I get it. You think I'm so hard up, that's what I gotta eat. Is that it?"

Allie stared at him. Why would he say such a thing?

Dub explained calmly, "We heard dogs barking when we were here before. The treats are for them."

As any *normal* person would have realized, Allie thought.

"Who says those dogs you heard were ours?" L.J. asked.

"Well, it sounded like they were in your barn," Dub answered. "Weren't they?"

"Maybe, maybe not. But say they were. They wouldn't need charity from you and Little Miss Fix-it."

Allie forced herself to stifle her anger. Why was L.J. being such a pain? Was he trying to hide something, or was he just too proud or too pigheaded to accept what he saw as "charity"? Or was he too smart to buy their story?

"My old man told you to get lost. So why'd you come back? What do you want?" L.J. demanded.

In L.J.'s experience, Allie realized, people didn't go out of their way to be nice unless there was something in it for them. She had to admit, this time he was right. She and Dub were after information. She had to figure out a way to get L.J. talking.

"Look," she said, holding the bag of biscuits by her side. "We're thinking of starting a business selling these things, and this is part of our marketing strategy. We're giving out free samples to everybody we know who has dogs, figuring that if the dogs like them, the people will come back to buy more. So, do you want them or not?"

L.J. shrugged, as if he didn't care one way or the other.

Allie decided to take this as a yes. She walked closer, stepped onto the porch, and set the bag down on top of one of the cardboard boxes. Dub followed right behind her.

An awkward silence fell. Allie didn't expect L.J. to offer them a seat or a glass of water or say or do anything that smacked of common courtesy, and he didn't. At least he no longer seemed to be giving off palpable waves of hostility. She told herself this was progress.

Then L.J. asked, "Where's the dog?"

The unexpected question flustered Allie. "What dog? Hoover? Oh, she's not mine," she answered, then mentally kicked herself. *Duh*. L.J. had first seen Hoover at school. "Well, you knew that," she amended. "I'm dog-sitting for Mr. Henry because he had to go away for a while."

L.J. waited for a second, then repeated, "So where's the dog?"

"Oh, she's home. I mean, at Mr. Henry's house. She can go in and out through her doggy door, and she's got a big yard to play in. I already fed her and took her for a walk, so she'll be okay until I go back."

Allie realized she was babbling and stopped herself. She wished L.J. didn't make her so nervous!

"How come you didn't bring her?"

Allie looked at Dub for help. She couldn't very

well admit that they had planned to sneak close enough to make sure that Mr. Cutler wasn't home, and had been afraid they wouldn't be able to keep Hoover quiet.

Dub answered. "She kind of flipped out on your dad, and he didn't seem to like her too much, either. So we thought it would be better to leave her."

L.J. nodded slightly, as if this made sense.

"So," Allie said, hoping to keep the conversation going, "what kinds of dogs do you have?"

A curtain seemed to fall over L.J.'s eyes for a moment. "Just dogs," he said. "No fancy breeds like that one the teacher's got."

"Oh, I like mutts," Allie said. "I like all dogs, really, but I can't have one because my brother's allergic. How many have you got? Could we see them?" She didn't seem to be able to stop chattering.

Something flickered in L.J.'s eyes, something Allie thought might be fear. "My old man doesn't like anybody going out there," he said.

Allie and Dub's puzzled expressions must have made L.J. realize that his comment required further explanation, because he added, "The dogs get all excited, and start barking, and next thing you know, the neighbors are complaining."

Allie gazed about. There were no other houses nearby, no neighbors to complain. She almost pointed this out, but stopped herself. L.J. wasn't going to take them to the barn, and Allie couldn't blame him. If she were in L.J.'s shoes, she wouldn't do anything to make her father mad, either.

But her dream had made it clear that there was a connection between that barn and her ghost, or between the barn and a dog named Belle.

She could mention Belle and see what happened. It was worth a try. "If I ever *did* get a dog," she said, "I'd get a female. I guess because I like Hoover so much and she's a girl. And I even know what I'd call her. Belle."

At that, L.J. jerked out of his slouching position as if he'd been stung. He sat up straight, all the color draining from his face. Just a few moments ago, Allie would have enjoyed seeing L.J. lose his cool, and been pleased to be the cause. But the expression on his face held so much pain that she had to turn away.

Before she could say or do anything more, Mr. Cutler's gray pickup truck appeared at the foot of Dundee Road, headed toward the house. Panic-stricken, Allie and Dub looked at L.J.

"You better get outta here," he said. He sounded worried and, worse, scared.

The truck neared the driveway and turned in, and the house blocked their view of it. For the moment, Mr. Cutler's view of them was blocked, as well. Allie and Dub ran across the yard, through the swamp, and into the shelter of the bushes. When they reached their bikes, they had to decide: should they stay hidden, or make a run for it on the open highway?

"Let's just get out of here," Allie said, panting. Dub nodded and jumped onto his bike.

Pedaling down the road, Allie looked back over her shoulder so often that she felt lucky not to crash. When she and Dub reached the edge of town with no sign of Mr. Cutler or his truck, they stopped.

"Man, that was a close one," Dub said, wiping the sweat from his face with his shirtsleeve.

"I think there's a chance he didn't see us," Allie said, gasping, "if he didn't look over at the porch when he was driving up the road. And he couldn't have seen us running across the yard because the house was in the way."

"Yeah," Dub answered, but he didn't sound convinced.

Allie caught her breath, then said, "Obviously, there's something in that barn L.J.'s father doesn't want us to see."

"Right. But if it's the dogs, I don't get what the big deal is," Dub said, looking puzzled.

"Maybe they're watchdogs or guard dogs," Allie said thoughtfully. "I doubt L.J. or his father is worried about the dogs hurting us. More likely, the dogs are there to scare people off and keep them from discovering whatever it is they're trying to hide."

Dub nodded. "Makes sense, I guess. What do you think they're hiding?"

Allie shrugged. "Drugs? Stolen stuff? I don't know. Something illegal."

"I don't get the connection between that and the ghost, though," Dub said.

"Me neither. But we definitely made one connection. Did you see L.J.'s face when I said the name Belle?"

Dub nodded, lifting his eyebrows. "You sure hit a nerve with that one."

"I wish I knew why."

"Maybe Belle's in the barn," Dub speculated.

"Maybe," said Allie. Then she reminded him, "But even though the ghost dog led me to L.J.'s house in the dream, the part about Belle seemed to take place somewhere else."

"The same place as your first dream, right? The mazelike place where the dog is whimpering?"

"Yeah," Allie said, feeling as if they were back to Square One. "It was a lot easier when the ghosts were human. They could talk to me, even write in my journal. But it's tough trying to understand these messages from a dog."

"I know," said Dub. He shrugged. "We're just going to have to be better detectives, I guess, and figure stuff out on our own."

Allie supposed he was right. There was something else she wanted to talk over with Dub. From the time she had met L.J. in Mr. Henry's classroom, she'd found him annoying. But for a brief moment on the porch, she had put herself in L.J.'s shoes. And now she was really trying to imagine being L.J., not for just a moment, but for every minute of every day. There was a lot that she couldn't know, or could only guess at, but she was pretty sure that being L.J. wouldn't feel too good.

She had no idea why her mention of Belle had upset him so badly, but she'd felt sorry when she saw his wounded expression. She tried to explain all this to Dub.

"Uh-oh," he said when she'd finished. "You want to go back, don't you?" He was pretending reluctance, but his eyes held a gleam of excitement.

"Of course," answered Allie.

"Tomorrow?"

"Yeah."

But something interfered with their plans. In the morning, when Allie pulled into Mr. Henry's driveway on her bike, the gate to the fenced-in pen was open. The yard was empty and so was the house. Hoover was gone.

Thirteen

Allie went over every inch of the house twice, then a third time, pleading with Hoover to come out of hiding and stop playing tricks.

"I mean it, Hoover," she called desperately. "This isn't funny."

She searched her memory: had she forgotten to shut the gate? No. She remembered carefully closing it and fastening the latch. And Hoover, brilliant as she was, didn't have the dexterity to unfasten it.

So what had happened? Perhaps some neighborhood child had seen Hoover and taken her out to play. Perhaps . . . *No!* She couldn't bear to think that any possible harm had come to Mr. Henry's beloved dog, especially when he had trusted Allie to care for her.

Finally she had to admit the truth: Hoover was gone. The reality of it rolled through her chest and down into the pit of her stomach, leaving a jittery sickness in its wake.

Crying, Allie picked up the phone to call her parents. She was shaking so badly she had to redial three times before she got the number right.

"Dad?" Thank goodness he hadn't left for work. "Dad, you've got to come, quick! Hoover's gone!"

Saying the words out loud caused a fresh burst of sobbing, and it took several moments before Allie had composed herself enough to explain.

"Stay there, Allie," her dad commanded. "I'll be right over."

While she waited, Allie continued to walk around the house in a state of disbelief, calling and cajoling. Soon the kitchen door burst open and her father, mother, and Michael all appeared. Her mother hugged her, while her father and Michael searched the house again, in vain.

When it was clear that Allie was right and Hoover had indeed disappeared, Mr. Nichols picked up the phone and called the police, who said they would be there as quickly as possible.

"Ann, you'd better get Michael out of here," said Mr. Nichols. "Look at him. Even with his pills, he's having a reaction from being in this house."

Michael sneezed then, as if any proof were needed beyond his red eyes and runny nose. But as Allie looked at her little brother, she saw in his eyes something more than allergic tears, and she knew what it was. Ever since she'd arrived at Mr. Henry's house, she'd felt the presence of her ghost.

"Come here, Mike," she said, indicating for him to follow her outside into the yard. She knelt beside him. "You feel it, too, don't you?" she asked.

Michael nodded. "Something bad is happening," he said, reaching up to rub the back of his neck.

"Does it feel prickly here?" Allie asked, touching the back of her own neck.

Michael nodded. Then he cocked his head, as if listening. "It's crying again, Allie. Do you hear it?"

"Yes," she whispered, more spooked than she'd ever been before.

"Can't you make it stop?" Michael asked plaintively.

"I'm working on it," she said. "In the meantime, don't listen if you can help it, and try not to worry."

Michael nodded, but he looked doubtful. Allie's heart went out to him. She thought about the dream she'd had, the one that Michael had not shared because he'd been fishing while she was napping, the dream in which she had felt the ghost dog leading her along. She was glad that Michael had missed *that*. She intended to protect him from as much unpleasantness as possible.

Michael was cocking his head again. "Now it's gone," he said.

Allie listened. He was right. The sounds inside her head were gone, too. "Yes," she said.

"But I heard something different, kind of like . . ." He paused, thinking, then smiled. "Like when I play drummer and bang on the pot with a spoon."

"Yes," said Allie. She had heard it, too, although she'd been so wrapped up in what she was saying to Michael that she hadn't paid close attention. She was vaguely aware that the sound was familiar, although she couldn't place it, and, besides, she had other, more pressing things on her mind.

The full horror of Hoover's disappearance came flooding through her once again. She was going to have to call Mr. Henry. He'd left an emergency phone number, saying that he was sure she wouldn't need it. Oh, how she wished she didn't!

She was interrupted in her dismal thoughts by a police car pulling into the driveway. A police officer Allie had seen directing traffic near school got out and introduced herself to Allie and her family as Officer Helen Burke.

After Allie explained exactly when she had last seen Hoover and what she had discovered that morning, the officer asked, "Are you certain that you latched the gate securely behind you last night?"

Allie said she was sure she had.

"Did you notice anything missing or disturbed inside the house?" Officer Burke asked next.

"No. The kitchen door was locked, the way I left it. The key is under that flower pot," she added, pointing. "Hoover gets in and out through the dog door."

Officer Burke nodded and said she was going to take a look around. When she'd inspected the house and yard to her satisfaction, she said, "Well, I don't see any reason to suspect foul play. No forcible entry, nothing missing other than the dog. It was probably kids, fooling around. All I can do is file a report at the station and alert the local shelter, in case someone turns her in. If someone does find her, it's good that her name and phone number are on the collar."

Seeing Allie's dismay, she added kindly, "Dogs go missing all the time. They almost always come back on their own once they've had their fun."

Allie hoped fervently that she was right.

They thanked Officer Burke, and Michael and Mrs. Nichols left to go home. Allie's father had driven over in his own car so that he could go straight to work from Mr. Henry's house. He stayed while Allie got up the courage to call Mr. Henry. The phone rang and rang, but there was no answer and no answering machine. Allie hung up. At first she was relieved, but then she wished Mr. Henry knew. Maybe he'd have a suggestion about where Hoover might go. And maybe Allie wouldn't feel so alone in her responsibility.

"Dad," she asked, "is it okay if I don't go home? If Hoover does come back, I should be here. I'll stay outside so I can watch for her, and I'll leave the window open so I can hear the phone in case somebody finds her and tries to call."

"That sounds like a good idea," said Mr. Nichols. "Call your mother to tell her. And call me at the office if you hear anything, okay, sweetie?"

"Okay."

"Don't worry, Allie-Cat. She'll turn up."

"Thanks, Dad," Allie answered, and her eyes filled with tears again.

She called to tell her mother of her plans, and Mrs. Nichols said she'd bring over some lunch after she took Michael to the baby-sitter. Then Allie called Dub and told him what had happened.

"I've got an idea," he said. "Hang on. I'll be there in a little while."

At first Allie paced the yard, looking in all directions and calling for Hoover. Soon, though, she merely sat on the kitchen step, feeling dejected and waiting for her mother and Dub to show up.

Mrs. Nichols came first, bringing sandwiches, chips, cookies, and drinks. "There's enough for Dub, too," she told Allie. "I thought he might be coming over to keep you company."

Allie nodded gratefully. "Thanks, Mom."

"I'll be at the store," Mrs. Nichols said. "Call if

you get any news, or if you just want to talk, okay?"

"I will."

Mrs. Nichols leaned down to give Allie a hug and whispered, "She'll turn up."

If enough people keep saying that, maybe it will come true, Allie told herself.

To her relief, it wasn't long before Dub pulled into the driveway on his bicycle. A bunch of papers fluttered from the clip attached to his rear fender. He pulled them free, and carried them over for Allie to see.

"What do you think?" he asked. "I made them up on the computer. I'd have made them fancier, but I didn't want to waste any time."

In huge letters at the top of each flyer was the word MISSING. Beneath that, in slightly smaller letters, Allie read, HAVE YOU SEEN THIS DOG? Underneath that was a photo. *My name is Hoover. I am a female golden retriever. I may be wearing a red collar with my name on it. Please return me to my owner.* Mr. Henry's address and phone number followed, along with Allie's home phone and both of her parents' work numbers.

"Wow, Dub," Allie said in amazement. "They're great. You thought of everything. But where did you get the picture?"

"Off the Internet," Dub answered.

"It looks just like her," Allie marveled.

"I kept looking until I found a good likeness," Dub said. "I figured it would help catch people's attention. So you want to go put them up?"

"I'd like to, but I think I should stay here in case she comes back."

"Oh, right. Okay, I'll go. I've got tape and thumb tacks in my backpack."

"Dub, thanks so much. You are the best." Allie felt dangerously near to crying again, and tried to get ahold of herself. "When you're done, will you come back here?" she asked. Pointing to the grocery sack her mother had left, she added, "I've got lunch."

"I'll definitely be back."

"Good." Allie watched him get on his bike and start off. "Thanks again," she called.

"No sweat," Dub called back.

Allie watched him go, feeling frustrated at the idea of doing nothing, yet knowing that she should be around in case Hoover returned. She decided that one thing she could do was ask the neighbors on either side of Mr. Henry's house and across the street if they had seen anything unusual going on.

No one was home at the house on the right. At the house on the left, a woman wearing a fuzzy purple bathrobe and matching slippers answered the door. "Don't tell me it's time for selling those cookies again," she said when she saw Allie. "I've still got some in the freezer."

It took Allie a second to realize the woman assumed she was selling Girl Scout cookies. She explained who she was and that Hoover was missing. "So I was wondering if you saw her this morning," she finished.

The woman shook her head. "But I heard her last night, barking her head off when I was trying to sleep. What a commotion!"

"Do you remember what time that was?" Allie asked.

The woman scrunched up her face in thought. "It must have been close to midnight, because I'd turned on the eleven-thirty movie." She shook her head in disgust. "Why people watch that stuff, I'll never know. It was pure rubbish. So I turned it off and got ready for bed. And that's when the ruckus started."

"Did you look over to see what was going on?" Allie asked.

"I mind my own business," the woman said with a sniff. "Anyway, I didn't have to look. I knew whose dog it was. So I called over there. I let the phone ring ten times, but there was no answer. Now you tell me Justin's away, which explains why he didn't come to the phone. But the barking stopped right after that. I figured he'd gone out and gotten the dog and taken her into the house. I went to sleep. There were no more disturbances after that. Until now," she added, peering narrowly at Allie.

"Oh!" Allie said. "I'm sorry! I didn't mean to bother you. I'm going now."

She turned and hurried down the path toward the sidewalk. The woman called after her, "Go see Muriel DiRaddo across the street. She's the busybody around here, not me."

Allie heard the door close, and when she peeked back she saw the curtain move at the window. The woman was apparently going to watch to see if Allie followed her suggestion. Allie's mouth twitched in a little smile as she crossed the street.

The man who answered Allie's knock wore the navy-blue uniform of the gas and electric company. The name Ozzie was sewn on the pocket. He smiled and said, "Can I help you, young lady?"

Allie introduced herself and explained that she was trying to find out anything she could about Mr. Henry's missing dog. The man turned and called loudly into the house, "Muriel!"

To Allie, he said, "My wife's the one to ask." He added proudly, "Muriel sees and hears *everything*."

When Muriel appeared, Ozzie gave her a peck on the cheek and said he had to be getting to work. Muriel pecked him back and turned to Allie. "Did I hear you say you're here about that dear boy's dog?"

Allie smiled. "Yes," she answered hopefully. "Hoover. Have you seen her?"

"*Well*," said Muriel, raising her eyebrows significantly, "not exactly. Not today, anyway."

"Oh," Allie murmured in disappointment.

"*But*," Muriel continued in a hushed voice, "I did hear her last night, and I said to Ozzie, 'Ozzie, something isn't right with that dog.' I knew Justin was away, of course, and at first I thought that poor animal was lonely. Now, I know you've been taking care of her, and doing a fine job, too. Nevertheless, she must miss her owner, don't you think?"

Allie nodded, surprised to realize that this woman had been observing her coming and going.

"But loneliness wasn't the problem, I'm quite sure of that," Muriel went on. "I've heard Hoover bark with joy and excitement, and sometimes she whines a little bit when Justin leaves for work. This barking was different. If I hadn't looked out the window and seen her, I wouldn't have believed it was Hoover. She sounded like a regular watchdog. Angry. *Ferocious*."

Allie listened, fascinated, as Muriel began to imitate the sounds Hoover had been making.

"So, naturally, I kept watching to see what was making her so upset."

Naturally, thought Allie wryly. Then she admitted to herself that she would probably have done the same thing.

"I stayed at the window for quite a while, but all I could see was that poor dog lunging at the fence. I went to another window to see if I could get a glimpse of what was bothering her, but I couldn't. Ozzie said it was most likely a skunk or a raccoon. I've smelled skunks in the neighborhood more than once, and I can tell you, I was hoping the dog hadn't gotten into one. Anyway, by then it was pretty late, and Ozzie likes a good night's sleep. So I pulled the curtain and went to bed. And not five minutes later, the barking stopped. Just like *that.*" Muriel demonstrated by snapping her fingers. Then she looked at Allie inquisitively. "But now you say the dog's missing?"

"Yes," Allie said, and all her worry and anxiety came back in a rush. She tried to control it, to think, and to ask the right questions. "You said she was lunging at the fence. She was in the yard, then?"

"Yes."

"And the gate was closed?" Allie asked.

Muriel nodded emphatically. "Just the way you left it. I could see that quite clearly."

Allie was relieved to have Muriel confirm that she had, indeed, closed the gate behind her. But her relief was quickly overtaken by dismay. Hoover hadn't found the door ajar and gone for an innocent romp around town. Someone had opened the gate.

Allie returned to Mr. Henry's house and checked

the answering machine to make sure no one had called to report finding Hoover while she'd been gone. The light wasn't flashing, but she hadn't expected it to be. She no longer believed she'd receive that call, nor did she expect the missing dog to return home on her own.

Her chest felt as if it were filled with fluttering moths, and she tried to calm herself. But there was no denying the direction her thoughts were taking. Hoover had to have been barking at a person, someone who remained carefully out of sight until Muriel left her post at the window. And then, when the coast was clear, that person had opened the gate and . . .

". . . *the barking stopped. Just like* that."

Allie forced herself to imagine what that might mean. She buried her face in her hands and sobbed.

Fourteen

When Dub returned, flushed from riding his bike all over town to post the flyers, Allie told him what she had learned.

He said, "You think someone took her?"

"Or—worse." Allie was barely able to get the words out. She kept imagining that she heard Hoover's frantic barking, followed by silence. What could that sudden quiet mean, except that— She couldn't bear to finish the thought.

Dub examined her face and seemed to hear what she was trying so hard to keep at bay. He said sternly, "Wait a second, Al. Just hold on. You may be right that someone took her. But there's no reason to think anything worse happened. It doesn't make sense. Why would a person sneak around at midnight and hide and all only to"—he paused and swallowed—"*kill* her? Or even hurt her. Think about it, Al. Really."

Allie looked at him, wanting to believe he was right.

He went on. "We might have a case of dog-napping here, but not murder. I mean, Hoover's a purebred golden retriever. She's a pretty valuable dog. I just don't see somebody going to all that trouble and then killing her, okay? Besides," he added excitedly, "I just realized something. If Hoover was dead, you'd know it. I bet her ghost would contact you right away!"

Allie nodded slowly. "I never thought of that," she said. "You could be right."

Dub looked relieved. "Okay, then," he said. "We're going to assume she's alive."

"But who would take her?" Allie wailed. "And why?"

They talked this over as they ate the lunch Allie's mother had left them. Allie only picked at her food, and she noticed that Dub didn't have his usual appetite, either. They tried to imagine what enemies Mr. Henry might have, and couldn't come up with any.

"And everyone who knows Hoover loves her," Allie said. Then, narrowing her eyes, she added, "Except L.J.'s creepy father."

"L.J. seemed awfully interested in her, too, remember?" Dub said. "At least he asked a lot of questions about her."

They pondered this as they stuffed the leftover food, wrappers, and cans back into the grocery sack.

"I'm going to call Officer Burke," Allie declared.

"Whoa," said Dub. "You can't just go around accusing people of dog-napping. I mean, you and I *suspect* L.J. and his father, but we don't have any *proof.*"

"I'm not going to accuse anybody," Allie answered. "I'm just going to tell her what Muriel said, and maybe mention that those guys were showing an unusual interest in the dog lately, and let her draw her own conclusions."

"I guess that would be okay," Dub agreed.

"And I should probably try to reach Mr. Henry again," Allie said hesitantly, half hoping Dub would try to stop her.

"Yeah," he said sympathetically.

"After that we might as well leave," Allie said, getting up to go inside.

Dub nodded. "There's no reason to hang around here."

Officer Burke wasn't at the station, but the desk sergeant said he didn't think there had been any reports about a dog being found. Allie explained to him what Muriel DiRaddo had seen the night before, and asked him to pass on the information to Officer Burke. With Dub's warning fresh in her mind, she didn't mention L.J.'s name or his father's, merely saying that she'd call back later, when Officer Burke was in.

Allie phoned Mr. Henry, but there was still no answer. Last, she called her mother at the store to tell her the news and to say they were leaving Mr. Henry's house to go to Dub's for a while. Mrs. Nichols had customers, so she couldn't talk long, but Allie promised to fill her in at dinner.

After she locked Mr. Henry's kitchen door, Allie and Dub pedaled slowly and dejectedly to Dub's house. As they drew near, they were surprised to see that someone was in the driveway, shooting baskets. Soon they were close enough to see that it was James. He was dribbling the ball furiously, as if he wanted to drive it into the asphalt. Then he made a quick series of shots, each time throwing the ball much too hard, so that it ricocheted wildly off the rim or the garage door. He'd chase it down only to make another crazy shot.

Allie and Dub pulled into the driveway just as James threw the ball at the garage door with all his might, making no pretense of taking a shot. The ball flew back toward the street, to where Allie and Dub had stopped their bikes at the end of the driveway.

James looked up, his expression first embarrassed, then defiant.

"Hi, James," Dub said somewhat uncertainly. "What's up?"

"Not much," James said. "I just quit the only job I could get around here, a job I really need, and now I don't know what I'm going to do. Other than that, everything's just terrific."

He reached down for the ball and held it at chest level with both hands, pressing hard, as if he were trying to pop it like a balloon. He didn't look at Allie or Dub, but off into the distance somewhere.

Allie and Dub exchanged bewildered glances, afraid to speak in the face of James's anger.

"You two still think you want to work for Enid?" he asked suddenly, turning toward them. "Well, don't say I didn't warn you."

"What do you mean?" Dub said.

"You want to know how my day began?" James demanded, tossing the ball toward Dub's house, where it disappeared under a bush. Without waiting for an answer, he said, "By discovering a dead puppy, that's how. There were only three left the last time you came in, right? Did you think the three missing ones went to wonderful, loving homes? Forget it. They died, then two more died. And I found the seventh one dead today."

James was crying now, his voice coming in harsh sobs that he hardly seemed aware of. " 'Luv'n' Pets'—what a crock!"

Allie was stunned. She was frightened and confused by the sight of an older boy crying and out of control and, at the same time, she felt completely sympathetic with his rage. All those cute puppies were *dead*?

"But what— I mean, how did they die?" she managed to ask.

James looked right at her then, his blue eyes blazing through a sheen of tears. "They come in sick half the time, and all Enid cares about is getting them cheap and selling them off before they croak on her. Did you ever notice how they're only in the window after I've been there in the morning? That's so customers won't walk by some evening and see dead or dying puppies. We keep them in the back room at night. Which is where I find them when I come in early to clean cages."

"That's awful," Allie said, hardly able to get the words out. "But why doesn't Enid take them to the vet if they're sick?"

James answered slowly, with exaggerated patience, as if Allie were dense or hard of hearing. "Because that would cost *money*. Which is the same reason they didn't get any veterinary care from the breeder—and I use the term loosely," he added darkly, "—in the first place. It's all about money. There's nothing 'luv'n' ' about it."

He shook his head, and it seemed to Allie that he was trying to dislodge unpleasant memories and make them go away. But now that he'd started, he appeared unable to stop describing the visions in his mind.

"This last litter was really bad. Usually a few pups live long enough for somebody to buy them. Then I can at least hope the owner is nice and responsible and will take care of them."

They were all silent for a moment. Then James went on bitterly. "Everybody sees the little balls of fur in the store and says, Oh, look how cute, but nobody thinks about where they came from or what might happen to them."

Allie cringed slightly, knowing that he was right. How many times had she been the person goo-gooing over the puppies in the window display?

"People don't want to see that it's a business, that people like Enid are in it for the money. They don't know she'll buy from any scumball who comes in the door saying he's got dogs for sale cheap. She doesn't ask questions about their breeding or how they were raised or if they had their shots. If they're cute and they're breathing, she might be able to sell them."

James's fury seemed to be spent. He gave a deep sigh, shoved his hands in the front pockets of his jeans, and kicked at the asphalt.

"Who knows about this besides you?" Allie asked after a moment had passed.

James shrugged. "There's people who know about it and are trying to stop it. I saw some stuff on the Internet. Around here, though, nobody seems to know or care."

"But aren't there laws about cruelty to animals?" Allie asked.

"Yeah. But you have to do something pretty outrageous. What most puppy mills do isn't against the law."

"Puppy mills?" Allie repeated. She'd never heard the term before. She didn't like the sound of it, and wanted to be sure she knew what it meant.

James sighed again. "Some guy keeps, say, ten or twenty—or fifty—dogs in his back yard in cages. The minute a female's old enough, he starts breeding her. As soon as possible after the first litter, he breeds her again. And again and again. That's her whole purpose in life: to make more puppies for the guy to sell. It isn't against the law. I read online about a few busts, like when somebody stumbled onto a really crummy operation, where there were lots of animals, and they were kept in small cages piled one on top of another so the dogs were messing all over the place, and they were dirty and sick and . . ." James's voice just petered out.

Allie felt sick herself. Also, she understood now that her ghost dog had been trying its best to make her see and even smell such scenes of misery. As James had been speaking, she had felt the familiar presence of her ghost the entire time.

Then James said something that made the little hairs on the back of her neck stand right on end.

"Oh, and you know that guy you were asking about? The one in the gray pickup? Well, he came back to talk to Enid. I tried to listen in on their conversation, but I only caught parts of it. I'm pretty sure he's going to be supplying her with puppies from now on. She used to get them from somebody in Pennsylvania, and she seemed thrilled that this guy is closer. It'll probably cost her less. I heard him talking about having a litter of purebreds soon. Enid ate *that* right up. I could almost see the dollar signs in her eyes."

James took his hands out of his jeans pockets. "Here," he said, giving something to Allie. "I took the guy's business card before I quit. You can keep it."

Allie and Dub examined the small, beige card. It looked old: the corners were bent, and it was slightly grimy. A printed line had been crossed out, and beneath it had been handwritten in blue ink *Fair View*

Farm. On the next line, in smaller type, was the name *Curtis Cutler*, followed by an address in Georgia, which also had been crossed out, and replaced by the address of the Cutler house on Dundee Road.

Dub made a face. "Not too classy," he said. "Guess old Curtis hasn't had time to get new cards printed yet."

"Look," Allie said, handing him the card after holding it up to the sunlight and squinting at it for a while. "The crossed-out part says Cutler Creek—something. I can't read the last word."

Dub peered closely at the black slash and shook his head. "Neither can I."

" 'Fair View Farm'?" Allie read out loud. "*That's* his name for the dump out on Dundee Road? Ha! *What* farm? *What* view?"

"It's a big, fat lie," said Dub.

"Kind of like the name Luv'n' Pets," Allie answered darkly.

Dub tried to hand the card to her, but she backed away. "I don't want it!" she said with disgust.

"I don't, either," Dub said, putting the card in his pocket. Then he smiled. "But it's a clue. It might come in handy."

Fifteen

Allie made sure Michael was busy riding his Big Wheel in the driveway before she poured out to her parents all the horrible things she had learned that day. Mrs. Nichols comforted Allie, who held back tears throughout her telling of the story.

Mr. Nichols dialed the police station and asked for Officer Burke. After a pause, he spoke into the phone. "Hello, Officer. Yes, I understand there hasn't been any news on your end. But I think you'd better listen to what my daughter has to say." He handed the phone to Allie.

Allie took a deep breath and said, "Hello, Officer Burke?" She carefully related every detail she could remember to make sure the police officer would understand that she and Dub weren't just a couple of crazy kids with overactive imaginations. She wanted the policewoman to see exactly how serious the situation was. "So," she finished, "we think L.J. and his father took Hoover, and we also think they could be operating one of those puppy mill places. Dub has his business card. We can show it to you."

She explained that the Cutlers lived on Dundee Road. When Officer Burke asked if Dub and Allie would accompany her there, Allie held her hand over the mouthpiece of the phone and said, "Mom, Dad. She wants to know if Dub and I can go to L.J.'s house after dinner with her and someone from the Humane Society. They want to look around and ask some questions."

Her parents glanced at each other. Mrs. Nichols said, "I don't know. What do you think, Bill?"

Mr. Nichols took the phone from Allie. "Hello, Officer. Isn't that kind of unusual, taking kids along on a complaint?"

He listened, nodding. "Oh. Uh-huh. I see. Well, then, I think it will be fine. You'll call Dub's parents, too? Okay, then. See you at seven."

After he hung up, he explained. "Apparently they do things like this all the time. Say a kid's bike is stolen and the kid claims he knows who took it. The police officer and the kid go to check it out. In this case, they'll say they had a report of a missing dog being seen in the area, and ask to look around. She doesn't expect any trouble."

Mrs. Nichols still looked concerned, but she said

to Allie, "I suppose you'll be safe with the police. Are you sure you want to do this?"

"Yes," Allie answered, although she wasn't absolutely, entirely sure.

Several minutes later the phone rang, and Dub spoke, sounding all fired up. "We're going to be in on a bust, Al! This is too cool!"

Allie had had a little more time than Dub to imagine ways in which it might not be so cool. For one thing, she was scared of Mr. Cutler and, she had to admit, of L.J. She'd already pictured herself facing them down, even with two officials and Dub at her side, and it was a daunting prospect. Worse, though, she couldn't even think about enjoying the thrill of it all until Hoover had been found.

She told Dub this. "Maybe I'll think it's cool when it's all over. Right now I have the heebie-jeebies. I just want Hoover safe at home."

"I'm not saying I'm not a little nervous," Dub admitted. "But I get so mad when I think of those dogs—"

"I know," Allie said miserably. "And poor Hoover in with them."

The very thought of it made her spine stiffen again in outrage. Dub was on the right track, she realized. Staying angry would help her to be brave. The cries and whimpers she continued to hear in her head helped, too.

"I keep remembering stuff L.J. said," she told Dub.

"Yeah," he answered. "Like when he asked Mr. Henry if he'd bred Hoover yet."

"And then he said she looked old enough," Allie added.

"Sure she is," Dub said gloomily. "If you plan to use her as a puppy producing machine."

"I keep hoping maybe we'll find that poor dog Belle I saw in my dream," Allie said.

"Unless she's the ghost," Dub reminded her gently.

They were both quiet for a minute after that. Then Allie said, "Dub, you know the worst thing? I keep remembering how I babbled all that stuff to L.J. about how Mr. Henry was away, and Hoover had her little fenced-in yard and her doggy door, and everything. Why didn't I just give him written instructions labeled 'Steal This Dog'?"

She felt guilt rising inside her, draining away her anger and strength, and was grateful when Dub said, "Cut it out, Allie. How were you supposed to know L.J. and his father were dog thieves and sicko dog breeders? I mean, until today, we'd never even heard about this creepy stuff."

Good old Dub. As usual, he knew the right things to say to make her feel better.

When she got off the phone, Michael came into the room, looking confused and a little frightened.

"Allie? It's crying again. Can't you make it stop?"

She gathered Michael into her arms and said, "It's going to be all right, Mike. It's going to stop tonight. So try not to worry, okay? The police are even going to help me. What do you think of that?"

Michael looked at her, his eyes wide, excited by the mention of the police. Allie went on. "Dub and I are going to ride in a police car to the bad place, and then everything will be okay." She hoped this was true.

"Can I come?" Michael asked eagerly.

"They can only take Dub and me this time," Allie told him.

Michael nodded, but his disappointment was evident. "Will they make the lights and the siren go?" he asked hopefully.

Allie laughed. "You can ask them when they come to get me."

During dinner, Allie tried to bolster her courage by thinking about Hoover, locked up somewhere, lonely and afraid, with no idea what was happening to her. It worked.

At seven o'clock, Michael was waiting on the front steps with Allie. He was the first one to spot the approaching police car, followed by a van with the words SENECA HUMANE SOCIETY written on the side in large yellow letters. He ran right up to the police car, shouting, "Can you make the siren go?"

Allie called into the house, "Mom! Dad! They're here!" Then she joined Michael.

When Allie's parents came out, Officer Burke introduced everyone to Ed McHugh, the driver of the Humane Society van. To Michael's delight, she let him sit in the driver's seat of the police car and turn on both the lights and the siren for a few seconds. She showed him how to say, "Roger. Ten-Four," into the radio. He stayed right there, turning the steering wheel and pretending to continue a conversation on the radio, while the grownups talked and Allie listened.

Officer Burke explained what was going to happen. "We'll go out there, say we're looking for a missing dog, and ask if they've seen it. We'll have to play it by ear from there, depending on how they react. If they cooperate, great. If they don't, we may have to go back with a search warrant. Right now, we're just looking for information." She smiled at Allie. "Okay. Are you ready?"

Allie climbed into the police car, and Michael reluctantly climbed out.

"Good luck!" called Allie's father.

Officer Burke drove to Dub's, with Ed McHugh following in the van. As they headed out of town and turned onto Dundee Road, she explained the plan again for Dub's benefit. Allie could feel her heart beating faster when they pulled into the driveway behind Mr. Cutler's gray pickup truck. She pointed out the barn to Officer Burke. "That's where we heard the dogs barking," she said. Then, wiping her damp palms on her shorts, she turned and gave Dub a shaky smile. "Here goes."

The four of them picked their way through the junk-strewn lawn and climbed the stairs to the porch. Officer Burke was lifting her hand to knock when the screen door opened and Mr. Cutler stood before them. To Allie's amazement, he said, "Well, what do you know? I was thinking of calling in a complaint on these kids, but must be somebody else beat me to it."

Allie felt her mouth fall open in astonishment. "A complaint against *us*?" she blurted. She looked at Dub, who looked just as incredulous.

L.J. appeared in the doorway then, standing slightly behind and to the left of his father. His face was a careful blank.

Officer Burke glanced at Allie and shook her head slightly, as if to tell her to keep quiet. Allie closed her mouth, and the police officer said pleasantly, "Mr. Cutler, I'm Officer Helen Burke. This is Ed McHugh, from the Humane Society, and I take it you already know these youngsters?"

Mr. Cutler's gaze swept contemptuously over Allie and Dub. "They were out here bothering my son, yeah. And they had a nasty dog with them. It went after me right on the main street of town. I got witnesses. That animal is dangerous and she can't control it, and I'd like to know what you people are going to do about it."

Ed McHugh looked confused, and Allie didn't blame him. She, too, felt off balance in the face of Mr. Cutler's accusations. Dub was staring at Mr. Cutler with narrowed eyes, his jaw jutting forward angrily. Officer Burke kept her expression neutral and continued speaking to Mr. Cutler. "Is the dog you're speaking of a female golden retriever wearing a red collar?" she asked.

"That's the one," Mr. Cutler declared.

"Well, actually, that dog is the reason we're here," Officer Burke continued. "She's been missing since about midnight last night, and we were wondering if you've seen her, or if you have any information on her whereabouts."

Allie's eyes met L.J.'s at that moment, and she thought she saw a flicker of fear there. She looked back at Mr. Cutler to see how he was reacting to the question. He had arranged his features into a perfect mask of surprised innocence. "Missing? Well, how about that? I haven't seen her, not since she attacked me on the street, anyway." He half turned to L.J. and asked, "How about you? You seen that dog around here anyplace?"

L.J. appeared startled at having been spoken to.

Then he quickly shook his head and muttered, "No."

Mr. Cutler looked back at the four of them standing on the porch and shrugged his shoulders. "We ain't seen her." Then he shook his finger at Allie. "I told you you'd better learn to control that animal. See what happens when you're careless?" He shook his head sorrowfully, as if at Allie's irresponsibility.

Allie was so amazed by the act the man was putting on for Officer Burke, and so angry, that she couldn't have spoken even if she'd been able to think of what to say. He had some nerve!

Mr. Cutler turned back to Officer Burke with a thin smile that made Allie think of a snake. "Well, Officer, you can be sure we'll let you know if we see the dog. Won't we?" he asked L.J.

L.J. nodded.

"So," Mr. Cutler said. "If that's all . . ." He paused, gesturing toward the stairs.

"We'll be going in just a moment, Mr. Cutler," Officer Burke said smoothly. "There's one more thing. We had a report that the dog might have been seen in this vicinity. We've also had a complaint about dogs barking out this way. So we'd like to take a look around, if you don't mind."

Mr. Cutler's snake-smile faltered for a moment, and he shot Allie a venomous glance before he said,

"We ain't got dogs. And who would be complaining if we did? There's nobody living out here but me and the kid."

So Mrs. Cutler *wasn't* there, Allie thought.

"Then you won't mind if we have a look around," Officer Burke was saying calmly.

Trying not to smile, Allie glanced at Dub. *Ha! Now we've got you, you lying creep!* She looked at L.J., who was staring at the floor, just as he had the morning his father had pushed him into Mr. Henry's classroom. It struck Allie that he was trying to be invisible. Once again, she had to resist the impulse to feel sorry for him.

Too late, L.J., she thought. *You're in it right along with your father. And now there's no place to hide.*

"We'll just go have a look in the barn," Officer Burke said. "It's possible the missing dog got in there somehow and can't get out. Then we'll be on our way."

Allie eyed Mr. Cutler nervously, sure that this was the moment when his phony act would crumble and he'd snarl at them to get lost. She cringed, waiting. But to her surprise, he gave an exaggerated sigh and said, "I told you, we ain't got dogs and there's nothing to see. But if you're determined to waste time at the taxpayers' expense, be my guest."

He started to close the door, but Officer Burke

stopped him. "Would you mind coming with us, sir?" she asked.

Allie wondered if the policewoman was worried about L.J. and his father escaping, or whether she didn't want Mr. Cutler accusing them of damaging his property when he wasn't looking, which seemed like the kind of thing he would do. In any case, it struck Allie as a good idea to keep an eye on L.J. and his father until they were handcuffed and on their way to jail—or whatever would happen after Hoover and the other dogs were discovered in the barn. Allie realized she didn't know.

Mr. Cutler shook his head in annoyance and rolled his eyes at L.J., as if the whole idea was too ridiculous to believe. As they walked toward the barn, Allie imagined Hoover's joy when she saw them, and she had to restrain herself from running ahead of everyone to release Hoover from whatever horrid cage she was being kept in.

As it was, Mr. Cutler reached the barn first, threw the door open defiantly, and motioned them inside. Then he stood back, crossing his arms against his chest.

Allie edged past him, through the dust motes that danced in the light from the open doorway, into the darkness of the barn. At first, she couldn't see anything. As she waited for her eyes to adjust to the dimness, she listened for a bark or a whine or a yip from the dogs. The silence was almost eerie. When she was able at last to see into the corners, she gasped in disbelief. Except for an old tractor and some tools, the barn was empty. There were no cages filled with puppy mill dogs living in desperation and misery. No Belle. No Hoover.

Allie turned to find Dub, but instead her eyes locked with Mr. Cutler's. He was staring right at her, his eyebrows lifted and his mouth twisted in a triumphant smirk. Allie shivered, and quickly looked away.

Sixteen

Officer Burke pulled a flashlight from her belt and shone it slowly around the inside of the barn, but Allie didn't even watch. She knew from Mr. Cutler's face that there was nothing to find. She looked at Dub, who appeared stunned, and L.J., who was still staring at the ground. She looked down, too, feeling like a balloon that had suddenly lost its air. Except that a balloon couldn't feel fury and humiliation, the way Allie did.

"Well, then," Officer Burke said slowly, "I guess we're finished here." She put the flashlight back in its place on her belt. "We'll be going now, Mr. Cutler. Sorry to bother you. Thank you for your time."

Mr. Cutler bared his crooked gray teeth, and Allie could see he was enjoying himself. "No problem, Officer," he said jovially. "We're always happy to help the police, aren't we, L.J.?"

L.J. mumbled something without taking his eyes off the ground, but Allie could tell that Mr. Cutler hadn't really been looking for an answer. He was having too much fun, now that he'd tricked the police and made fools of her and Dub.

She tried to catch Dub's eye, but he was back at the barn door, sniffing loudly. Allie couldn't imagine what he was doing.

But then Dub said, "Wait a second!"

All faces turned expectantly in his direction.

"Take a whiff in here and tell me what you smell," Dub said to Officer Burke.

She looked at him, her expression half-curious and half-annoyed.

"Please," Dub added.

Officer Burke sighed, stepped back into the barn, and took several deep sniffs. "Pine," she said finally. "Like floor cleaner."

"Exactly!" said Dub, looking extremely pleased with himself.

Allie wondered briefly if he was losing his mind. "Dub," she urged, "what's your point?"

"What barn smells like pine?" Dub asked. Then, answering his own question, he said, "A barn that's been cleaned out and disinfected to hide the smell of the dogs that were cooped up inside." He looked around triumphantly.

"This is ridiculous," Mr. Cutler muttered. To Officer Burke, he said, "You gonna lock me up for having a clean barn?"

The officer gave him a hard look and said only, "I think we're finished here."

"But—" Allie began.

Officer Burke shot her a look almost as fierce as the one she'd given Mr. Cutler, and Allie closed her mouth.

"Come on," Ed McHugh said tersely. "Let's go."

As they all walked toward the driveway where the police car and van were parked, Mr. Cutler said, "You say that missing dog was seen out this way? A vicious animal like that—" He broke off, shaking his head. "Well, I just hope you find her before she hurts somebody."

Allie could feel the man's eyes on her, but she refused to look at him. She could just imagine the sly pleasure she'd see in his face. He was baiting her, and she wasn't about to give him the satisfaction of responding.

But there was something else that kept her quiet. There was something about his cockiness that was making her extremely uneasy. He was lying through his teeth: she knew it, Dub knew it, and L.J. knew it. But Mr. Cutler didn't seem to have any fear of being caught. His confidence was puzzling—and frightening. It made him seem capable of almost anything.

Allie hoped both of the Cutlers would leave them

and go back to the house, but Mr. Cutler accompanied them to the police car, and L.J. followed. Several times, Allie had sneaked little peeks at L.J., and every time his face had been the same empty, careful mask. He wasn't gloating, but he certainly didn't seem bothered by the blatant lies. It wasn't that she expected L.J. to speak out against his father, as afraid as he obviously was. But part of her wanted to believe L.J. was as disgusted as she was by Mr. Cutler's behavior.

Allie told herself she was being ridiculous. She'd known L.J. was trouble the first time she'd laid eyes on him at school, and he'd never done anything to change her mind. Like father, like son. They were in it together.

She got into the back seat of the police car next to Dub, rather than sit up front with Officer Burke, who had undoubtedly had it with them both. Allie and Dub watched as Ed McHugh shook hands with Mr. Cutler and said good night to Officer Burke. Then the Humane Society officer leaned into the rear of the car and said, "Next time, you kids get your facts straight before you waste adults' time, you hear?" He didn't wait for an answer before getting into the van, and Allie felt far too demoralized to speak, anyway.

Officer Burke got into the car and started the engine. Before they pulled away, Mr. Cutler said to her,

"No harm done, Officer. You know kids. They get wild ideas sometimes. What are you gonna do?" He shrugged. "I'll even forget my complaint against this young lady, seeing as how she probably feels bad enough about the dog being missing and all."

Officer Burke nodded and said, "Good night, Mr. Cutler." As they pulled away, Allie forced herself to look back. Mr. Cutler had turned and was heading to the house, but L.J. was standing in the driveway watching them leave. She had an odd thought: *He's home, but he looks lost.*

After she had turned from Dundee onto the road leading into town, Officer Burke finally spoke. "Well," she said, "that didn't exactly go the way we expected."

"What do we do now?" Dub asked. "Get a search warrant?"

Allie looked at him in amazement. Didn't he understand that Mr. Cutler had outfoxed them? They were, at best, two kids whose imaginations had gotten out of hand. At worst, they were troublemakers lodging false accusations against innocent citizens. Either way, the police wouldn't want any more to do with them.

"We have no reason to get a warrant," the officer replied, sounding surprised. "He let us look around. There was nothing to see. And we can't arrest him because his barn smells too clean."

"So that's it?" Dub protested. "The guy was lying!"

"You mean about Hoover attacking him?" Officer Burke asked.

Dub rolled his eyes in frustration and Allie answered this time. "Hoover doesn't like him," she admitted. "But she just barked at him. She never *attacked* him."

"He said you two were out there bothering his son. What was that about?"

Allie and Dub looked at each other. Allie imagined saying, *Well, you see, a ghost dog led me there in a dream.* Instead, she said, "We told Mr. Henry we'd try to make friends with L.J.—that's the son—because he came at the end of the year and didn't know anybody. So we did."

Officer Burke was quiet for the rest of the drive. When they pulled up in front of Dub's house, she turned around to face Allie and Dub. "I don't understand exactly what is going on here," she said. "But I'm advising you to stay away from the Cutlers. Hoover isn't there, and I didn't see anything to back up your theory about a puppy mill. We have no reason to bother those people any further. Do you understand?"

Allie and Dub nodded silently.

Officer Burke sighed and pushed a lock of hair off her forehead. Speaking kindly but firmly, she said,

"Listen, I know you believed what you were saying. But it's serious business to accuse a person of theft. And there is simply no evidence. You've got to drop this now. Agreed?"

Allie and Dub nodded again.

"All right, then," she said. "Good night, Dub."

Dub got out of the car, reached into his pocket, and handed Officer Burke Mr. Cutler's business card. "Maybe this isn't proof," he said, "but we think it might be a clue."

Officer Burke examined the card. "Thank you, Dub," she said. "I'll look into it."

Allie watched Dub walk up the driveway to his house. The slump of his shoulders told her he felt as discouraged as she did. The way he kicked at a spot on the asphalt meant he, too, was thinking, *But this isn't right. He was lying!*

When Officer Burke and Allie got out of the car in front of the Nicholses' house, Allie's parents were working in the flower gardens out front, and Mike was riding his Big Wheel in the driveway. He jumped off and ran toward the car, and Allie's parents came over, too.

"Well, how did it go?" asked Mr. Nichols as Michael climbed into the front seat, making his own siren noises. Officer Burke didn't answer, waiting for Allie to respond.

"From the looks on your faces, not too well," said

Mrs. Nichols, glancing anxiously from Allie to Officer Burke and back.

"Not too well," Allie echoed glumly.

"Was he uncooperative?" Mrs. Nichols asked.

Allie didn't answer, and after a moment, Officer Burke said, "No. He let us look around. But we found no sign of Hoover or any other dogs."

Allie's mother arched her eyebrows questioningly, waiting to hear the rest of the story. Officer Burke said, "Allie? Will you excuse us for just a minute? I'd like to talk to your parents."

In a dull voice, Allie said, "Sure."

"Michael, go inside with Allie and get a drink," Mrs. Nichols said, looking worried now.

Allie trudged up the walk with Michael, trying to hold back a sudden rush of tears. *Here we go again,* she thought. Once again, her parents were going to think that her overactive imagination was getting her into trouble. Once again, she couldn't explain herself without saying that she was responding to a ghost. Not only that, but a ghost *dog*. It wasn't an explanation that was likely to calm her parents' fears.

She poured Michael a glass of lemonade. He took a sip, then said, "You told me everything would be okay after you went to the bad place. But I still smell the poopy smell." He sniffed. "And it's still crying. Don't you hear it, Allie?"

Allie paused to concentrate and realized that

Michael was right. She knew she hadn't fixed anything by taking the police to the Cutlers' house, but she'd been so frustrated by Mr. Cutler that she hadn't paid attention to the faint but persistent sound of whimpering in her head. It was almost like background music, easy to ignore when she had other things on her mind.

And the "poopy" odor. Yes, she smelled it now. It was the smell she'd expected to find at the Cutlers' barn. She hadn't even realized she'd been smelling it until Michael mentioned it.

But so what? She had seen for herself: the barn was empty, and Mr. Cutler had cleaned away all the evidence.

Over the rim of the glass of lemonade, Michael's eyes looked frightened, and Allie didn't know what to tell him to make him feel better. Hoover was still missing, and she had no idea where to look. She was no closer to helping her ghost rest in peace. She had accomplished exactly nothing, except to alienate the police, upset her parents—and give Mr. Cutler a good laugh.

Seventeen

Later, Allie was lying in bed, exhausted but too wired to sleep, when her mother came in.

"Al? Are you awake?"

"Um-hmm."

Mrs. Nichols sat on the edge of the bed and gently smoothed Allie's hair. "I'm sorry about the way things went, sweetie," she said.

"I know, Mom," Allie mumbled.

"You want so much to find Hoover safe and sound. It's easy to see how you could take a few bits of information, put them together, and come up with an answer, even if it was the wrong answer."

Allie held back a sigh. She knew what her mother was going to say, and she couldn't blame her, really.

"But promise me you'll do as Officer Burke asked, and stay away from those Cutlers. From what Officer

Burke said, Mr. Cutler seems to have taken a dislike to you, and he sounds like a good person to avoid."

Allie was saved from answering by her father's appearance at the door. "Al, I tried Mr. Henry's number again, but there's still no answer. It's just as well, really. There's nothing he can do from out there, and knowing Hoover is missing will only make him worry."

Her father was right. It was awful knowing about Hoover and being helpless to find her. "Thanks, Dad," she said.

"I'm hoping by the time we do reach him, we'll have good news to report," Mr. Nichols went on.

Allie wanted to believe this, but she no longer could.

"The police know their job, honey," said her mother. "Officer Burke assured us she intends to continue working on this."

How is she going to catch Mr. Cutler if she's already decided he's innocent? thought Allie. But she didn't say anything. What was the point?

"Good night, Allie-Cat."

"Try not to worry."

"Okay. Night, Dad. Night, Mom."

The door closed, and she lay in the dark, trying not to worry. It was like trying not to breathe. She was sure she'd never sleep again.

But she must have drifted off at some point, because she was suddenly startled awake. Had she heard an odd noise, or dreamed it? She glanced at the clock on her bedside table. It said 1:17 in the morning. She lay still, listening. Then—there it was again, a rattling at her window.

She got up slowly, walked over to the window, and peered out, wondering sleepily if it was hailing outside. Or maybe a crazy squirrel was cracking open nuts, or— She couldn't imagine what else might be making the sound.

In the tree-shadowed yard below her window, she made out the shape of a person. She sucked in a quick breath of fear before she saw the outline of a bicycle lying in the grass. The person was about her size. Dub!

Good old Dub! He must have had a brainstorm in the night. He had a plan, and now he was here to get her so they could carry it out.

Hastily, she pulled her nightgown over her head, threw on some jeans, a T-shirt, and her sneakers, and quietly inched her bedroom door open. No squeaks—good. Reflecting that for once she was glad she didn't have a dog that might bark and alert her parents, she tiptoed toward the stairs. When she passed Michael's room, she could see his small, sleeping form in the glow from his X-Man night-light. She paused to cock her ear toward her parents' room at the far end of the hallway. Light, regular snoring sounds came from the open doorway.

Gingerly, she placed a foot on the far right edge of the first step, knowing how the old stairs creaked when she and Michael pounded up and down in the middle. Slowly, step by careful step, she made her way down. Only once was there a groan of wood against wood, which caused her to freeze in panic. But her parents never stirred. Heart hammering, she reached the bottom, slipped out the front door, and ran through the damp grass to the side of the house, where Dub was waiting under her window.

But when she drew close, her pounding heart leaped right into her throat. The person facing her wasn't Dub. It was L. J. Cutler.

Before she could scream or shout for help, L.J.'s hand moved quickly to cover her mouth.

"If you promise to keep quiet," he whispered fiercely, "I'll take my hand away."

Allie managed to nod. She was so paralyzed with fear, she didn't think she'd be able to speak, anyway. Her mind was whirling with questions and wild ideas about what in the world L. J. Cutler was doing at her house in the middle of the night.

L.J. looked right into her eyes for a long moment before he removed his hand. Allie, free now, remained still and stared back. Something passed between them during that short time. Allie wasn't sure what it was, but her heart slowed its frantic pounding, and she felt her fear subside.

"What are you doing here?" she asked quietly.

"I'm gonna help you get your dog back."

"You took her! I knew it!"

L.J. shook his head impatiently, but said only, "And there's something you gotta do for me."

Allie looked into his dark eyes. "What?"

"You'll find out. Come on." L.J. bent to pick up the bicycle that lay on the grass, and Allie was surprised to see it was the same pink bike she and Dub had stepped over in the Cutlers' yard. She'd assumed it was broken. Maybe it had been, and L.J. had fixed it. Ordinarily, she might have found it amusing to see L. J. Cutler mounting a pink bicycle with tattered pink and purple streamers on the handle grips. But there was nothing ordinary about this night.

"Where are we going?" Allie asked.

"You'll see. Just follow me. *Hurry.*"

"All right. Let me get my bike," said Allie. But if L.J. was going to issue ultimatums, she had a demand of her own. "We've got to get Dub. His room's on the first floor. It'll be easy to wake him up."

"No! There's *no time*!"

"I'm not going without Dub," Allie said, crossing her hands over her chest. Part of her was amazed at her own courage in standing up to L.J. Maybe it wasn't courage. Maybe she was afraid, and that was why she wanted Dub along. At any rate, it didn't feel right to go without him.

"He can help," she added.

L.J. let out an angry breath. "All right. We'll get your boyfriend—"

"He's not my boyfriend!" Allie protested.

"*Would you just get your bike,*" L.J. said, sounding exasperated. "I *told* you, there's *not much time*."

Allie ran to the garage, entering by the small side door instead of lifting the heavy, noisy garage door. L.J. was already at the end of the driveway, ready to go. She rode up, motioned for him to turn left, toward Dub's house, and followed him out onto Cumberland Road.

It almost didn't seem real, to be pedaling her bike quickly down the middle of her silent street in the quiet summer darkness. A half-moon gave enough light to see by. The moist air still held the day's heat, and Allie almost felt part of the night itself.

They didn't pass a car or a single soul, adding to the dreamlike feeling of their trip. When they reached Dub's house, Allie was relieved to see that he'd left his bike leaning against the porch. She got off her own bike, motioned for L.J. to stay where he was, and went around to the back of the house, where Dub's room was. The window was open, the curtains fluttering slightly in the night breeze.

She looked in and saw Dub lying on his back, his legs sticking out from under the sheet. She scratched on the screen and whispered, "Dub! Get up! It's me."

There was a slight rustle from the bed, as if Dub had awakened and was wondering, as she had, if he'd really heard something or merely dreamed it.

"Dub!" she whispered again. "Wake up! It's me."

Dub sat up and looked toward the window. "Allie?" he said groggily, throwing off the sheet. He was wearing a T-shirt and baggy boxers.

"Shhh!"

"What are you doing here?"

"Quiet. I'll tell you in a minute. Come on out."

"Out the *window*?" Dub asked. He didn't seem to be fully awake.

Allie thought about it. The window looked big enough, and it was probably safer than trying to get through the house without waking his parents. "Yeah."

Dub came over and started lifting the screen.

Allie almost laughed. *"Put some clothes on,"* she said. "And some shoes."

Dub scratched his head, then shook it a few times to wake himself up. By the time he'd pulled on shorts and sneakers and slid out the window to stand beside Allie, there was a big grin on his face. "So what's up?" he asked.

"L.J.'s here, too."

Dub's smile fell. "L.J.'s *here*?" he repeated.

"He says he'll help us find Hoover. And we have to do something for him."

"What does he want us to do?"

"I don't know," Allie answered. They were both still whispering. "But I didn't have much choice. We've got to get Hoover back. Anyway, we have to hurry. L.J.'s really jumpy. He keeps saying there's not much time."

"I'm glad you came to get me."

"Me too."

"Let's go."

Eighteen

L.J. was out the driveway and heading down the road as soon as Allie and Dub appeared at the front of Dub's house, and they had to pedal hard to catch up with him. He led them on a familiar route, and at first Allie thought he was taking them back to his house. But he slowed down at the entrance to the old bean packing plant and turned into the driveway. He stopped right there, and moved his hand up and down in a signal to Allie and Dub to be very quiet.

"The teacher's dog's here," he said in a tense voice. "There's a bunch of other dogs, too. My old man's home. He's pretty drunk, but his hearing's great. If all them dogs start barking, the sound's gonna carry up the hill on a night like this."

Allie was trying to take in what L.J. had said, and figure out what it meant.

"What are we supposed to do?" Dub asked.

"I'm gonna get the old man's truck and come back here," L.J. said.

"You're going to *drive*?" Allie asked in amazement.

"Yeah," L.J. answered impatiently.

"You know how to *drive*?"

L.J. shrugged. "I figured it out. Sometimes the old man gets too blasted to see, forget about driving. So I take over. It ain't so hard."

"Oh." Allie tried to hide her astonishment, as if having to take the wheel because her father was too drunk to drive were something that happened to her every day.

"So listen," L.J. said urgently. "You two stay here till I get back, but you can't make *any* noise, you got it?"

Allie and Dub both nodded.

"Then we'll start loading the truck."

"With what?" Allie asked, but even as she said it she knew the answer.

"The dogs," said L.J. "Nine of 'em, plus a litter, plus that one of yours."

"But—" Allie began.

"I know it," L.J. said, his dark eyes growing even darker. "The racket'll be enough to wake the dead, and my old man, too, probably. But I'll have his wheels, and he don't run so fast anymore. We drive to the police station, and it's all over."

Allie nodded. L.J. had clearly thought the whole thing through. He was going to turn his father in to the police. She could hardly believe it. It struck Allie as a very brave—or very foolhardy—thing to do. But then she had a thought.

"L.J.," she asked, "if you want to stop what your father's doing, why didn't you say something when we came to the house with the police? Or call the police sometime when your father was out?"

L.J. shook his head. Allie didn't know if he considered her question too stupid to answer or whether he just didn't feel like explaining. In the faint light, he looked tired as he pushed the pink bicycle forward with his foot and rode away.

She and Dub looked at each other, too dumbfounded to speak and afraid, now that L.J. was heading home, of alerting the dogs and waking Mr. Cutler just as L.J. was taking the truck.

Allie's brain buzzed with all the things that could go wrong. What if Mr. Cutler had gotten up to use the bathroom and found L.J. missing? What if he heard L.J. start up the truck? What if this was all a trick, and L.J. was setting them up?

She began to feel very frightened. She strained to listen for any sound coming from Dundee Road, but the night was quiet except for an occasional hollow tap, when the loose flap of metal on the old roof of the bean plant lifted and fell in the slight breeze.

Now she knew: that was the sound she and Michael had heard in their heads, a message from the ghost dog. They must have heard it at the very moment when Mr. Cutler was moving the dogs, including Hoover, to the bean plant so they wouldn't be discovered on his property.

There was so much she didn't understand about what was happening. First of all, what had made L.J. decide to help her? But right behind that puzzling question were others. What would happen to L.J. if his plan failed? Mr. Cutler would be furious.

Then Allie realized that it was just as frightening to imagine what would happen to L.J. if his plan succeeded. Either way, he was certain to be in big trouble with his father. Allie had seen Mr. Cutler's anger over a bad cut in a piece of plywood. She didn't want to think about what he would do to L.J. for this.

Dub's face looked troubled, and she figured many of the same thoughts were going through his head. The wait seemed to be taking forever. Where was L.J.? Shouldn't he be back by now? Had he been caught? Did he really know how to drive? She closed her eyes, focusing every nerve and muscle on listening. Then, there it was, the sound of the truck slowing at the corner and turning. Lights out, it approached the place where she and Dub stood, still straddling their bikes.

"Ditch the bikes for now," L.J. said softly through

the open driver's side window. "Hide 'em someplace and come on."

Allie and Dub hid their bikes in some overgrown bushes and made their way back across the parking lot, where weeds poked up through the buckled asphalt. L.J. had parked the gray pickup close to what Allie figured was the old loading dock. He jumped out of the front seat, leaving the door open, then reached into the truck's cab and took out several lengths of rope. He handed them to Dub, and gave Allie a wad of rags and an empty burlap sack. L.J. held a flashlight and another sack with something in it. He motioned for Allie and Dub to follow him.

Inside the walls of the plant, L.J. switched on the flashlight for just a moment, allowing him to get his bearings and giving Dub and Allie a chance to get a glimpse of the layout. After the flashlight went out, Allie was surprised to feel L.J. take hold of her arm. She, in turn, grabbed Dub's arm and the three of them inched their way silently through the solid blackness.

Since she was unable to see, Allie's sense of smell seemed stronger than usual, and the dank odor of decay that had wafted from the plant during the day was almost overpowering. Beneath it was the smell Michael had identified as "poopy."

Allie hoped that Michael was deep in sleep at that moment, and not experiencing a frightening dream or ghostly sensation, especially without her there to comfort him. But she couldn't think about that now. She had to concentrate on shuffle-stepping silently behind L.J. through the blackness, and keeping her grip on Dub. Suddenly, there was a loud metallic clang as L.J. walked into something lying on the floor. He fell, letting go of Allie's arm in the process.

In the quiet afterward, Allie heard L.J. swear softly. Then there was a whimper, followed by a sharp bark, then another, and another. The sound echoed through the empty plant, seeming to tear right through the black fabric of the night. L.J. swore again, and turned on the flashlight. He stood up, disentangling his foot from between the rungs of an old aluminum ladder.

"We gotta be quick now," he said urgently. Leaving the flashlight on, he began to run, and Allie and Dub ran along behind him through one huge, yawning room and down a corridor to another room, where the barking had risen to a howling chorus.

There were the dogs, some in wire cages, some chained to posts driven into the earth floor, all of them barking, whining, and yelping in earnest now. At first, in the wildly swinging beam of the flashlight, it was hard to tell how many there were—the noise was so deafening it sounded like hundreds!

Allie saw scattered about a few aluminum pie

plates, which must have been used for food or water. The smell here was strong, as the dogs had been forced to relieve themselves where they were. It was the smell Mr. Cutler had worked so hard to hide in his barn.

The flashlight shone for a moment into a corner and Allie let out a cry. She raced to the wire cage, felt for the latch, fumbled with frantic fingers until it opened, and threw her arms around Hoover. Hoover bathed her face in kisses.

Allie's joy was interrupted by L.J., who came up behind her and said angrily, "There's no time for that! Give me some of those strips." Allie held out her hand and he took some of the pieces of cloth. "Get going. We gotta muzzle 'em all, quick," he said, "before they make any more noise."

At Allie's uncomprehending look, he took one of the strips of cloth, looped it over Hoover's nose, twisted it under her chin, and tied the ends behind her neck, making it impossible for her to bark.

L.J. had propped the flashlight on the ground, and in the arc of light that spread across the floor, Allie could see that he had taken biscuits from the sack he'd been holding and scattered them about. The food kept the dogs quiet while he and Dub busily tied the cloth strips around the muzzle of one dog after another.

Allie helped, noticing that the dogs were of different breeds and different sizes. Most were noticeably pregnant.

"Take that empty sack," L.J. ordered Allie. "Wait until I get the mother muzzled, then put her puppies in it."

Allie saw that beneath the dog L.J. was muzzling was a litter of tiny, squirming puppies, so young their eyes weren't yet open. "Put them in the sack?" she repeated uncertainly.

"Do it!" L.J. said, sounding exasperated. Allie, realizing this was no time to be overly delicate, lifted the tiny, warm bodies and placed them inside the sack. The mother pawed frantically at L.J. as she watched her puppies being taken and, even muzzled, she was able to whine her distress.

"Where's that rope?" demanded L.J.

Dub pointed to the floor, where he'd set the rope while putting on muzzles.

"Okay, tie a piece around each one's neck," L.J. said, handing three lengths of rope to Dub, three to Allie, and keeping the rest for himself.

When all the dogs were leashed, L.J. spoke again. "I'll take four dogs and the sack. You each take three dogs—you, take that one," he said to Allie, indicating Hoover. "We'll head for the truck as fast as we can and load 'em in the back. Let's go."

L.J. had his hands full with four dogs and the sack

of puppies, so Dub led the way, holding the flashlight. This time, they made no attempt to tiptoe quietly. They moved as quickly as they could while herding ten confused, frightened, and uncooperative dogs in a tangle of leashes.

If Mr. Cutler had heard the dogs barking, he was already on his way. There wasn't a moment to waste.

The parking lot was empty except for the gray pickup. The bed of the truck was covered with a cap, making it a little like a small camper. L.J. opened the tailgate, lifted the first dog, and put it inside. When he turned to pick up a second dog, the first jumped out of the truck.

"We don't have time for this!" L.J. muttered furiously.

Allie listened for any sound of Mr. Cutler approaching, but couldn't hear anything except the shuffling and muffled whining of the dogs. She moved forward to block one side of the tailgate opening and Dub moved to the other, so the dogs L.J. loaded couldn't jump out while he was loading the others. It seemed to take forever, but finally all ten were squeezed in.

"You hold the pups on your lap," L.J. told Allie, thrusting the sack into her arms. "Come on, get in."

Allie climbed into the front of the truck, sitting awkwardly in the space between the two seats. She opened the top of the sack so the puppies could breathe, and balanced it as gently as she could on her lap. L.J. and Dub got in on either side of her. Then, as if he'd been driving all his life, L.J. threw the gearshift into reverse, and they were backing away from the loading dock.

They had done it! They had the dogs and were on the way to the police station!

L.J. stopped, put the truck in forward gear, turned the wheel, and began heading for the parking lot's exit onto the road. He leaned forward, feeling for the headlights, and switched them on.

Suddenly, as if he had materialized out of the night itself, Mr. Cutler stood directly in the path of the truck, hands on his hips, head back, eyes narrowed against the glare. Behind him, the pink bicycle lay on its side in the gravel. Allie gasped, Dub shouted "Hey!", and L.J. slammed on the brakes.

Nobody moved or spoke for what felt like a long while. Then Mr. Cutler's voice came through L.J.'s open window.

"Just what you think you're doin', boy?" He spoke slowly, as if he had all the time in the world. His words were slightly slurred, it seemed to Allie, but he stood steadily on his own two feet. He was shaking his head mockingly, as if he already knew the answer to his question and found it pitiful.

"You know what I'm doing and you better not try to stop me." L.J. sounded as if he was choking, and

Allie was horrified to see tears running down his face.

Mr. Cutler let out an ugly laugh. "You gonna run me down?"

"If I have to."

"Look at you. You're cryin'. Ya got snot all over your face."

"Get out of the way," L.J. warned, his voice shrill.

"Your mother tried to pull something like this one time. She didn't get away with it, and you won't, either."

"But she got away from *you*, finally, didn't she, old man? And I aim to, too."

"This is about that dog, isn't it? Your precious *Belle*?" Mr. Cutler said the name as if it tasted nasty in his mouth. "I am so tired of this crap. How many times I told you? If we're gonna eat, I gotta work. My business is dogs. Sometimes dogs die. It's the way it is."

"She didn't just *die*!" L.J. screamed, sobbing now with fury. "You *killed* her!"

"You little pain in my butt. That's it." And then, so quickly Allie didn't know how he did it, Mr. Cutler had moved from the front to the driver's side of the truck. His arm snaked through the window and around L.J.'s neck. With his other hand, he seemed to be struggling to open the door.

L.J. stomped on the gas pedal with all his might,

and the truck lurched forward. There was a crunch of metal as they ran over the bicycle. Mr. Cutler's arm still encircled L.J.'s neck, and he was forced to run along next to the truck, his neck bent to the side, while L.J., his own head halfway out the window, steered crazily with one hand and pushed at his father's face with the other.

They careened toward a pair of stout metal poles that had once held a sign marking the entrance to the plant. Allie screamed and grabbed the wheel, pulling it sharply to the right. L.J.'s foot seemed to be frozen all the way down on the gas pedal, and the truck veered in a tight circle. The engine roared and the tires spewed gravel.

Allie pounded on Mr. Cutler's arm with her fists, but it didn't have any effect, and she was afraid she was hurting L.J. more than his father. The truck continued to race in wild circles. Mr. Cutler was shouting and swearing, trying to keep his footing while his body was hanging from L.J.'s neck, and Dub was leaning across Allie to hold on to the steering wheel.

Allie looked at the bare skin of Mr. Cutler's arm around L.J.'s neck and did the only thing she could think of. She leaned over and bit down hard.

There was a screech of pain and outrage, and Mr. Cutler's arm slid from around L.J.'s neck. L.J. straightened up, held tightly to the wheel, and turned out of the parking lot and onto the road, still going very fast.

Dub opened his window, stuck his head out, and looked back. "He's just standing there, rubbing his arm," he said. "He can't catch us now."

It took a moment before L.J. was able to communicate that news to his foot. He slowed down at last, and they continued none too steadily down the long, straight, deserted stretch of road that led into town. They were all far too shaken to talk. The muzzles must have come off a couple of the dogs because frantic barking sounded from the back, and the puppies were whimpering and squirming in Allie's lap. Allie felt like whimpering, too.

L.J. turned when they reached the main crossroad in town. There were no other cars about, and the town center had an eerie, lonely feel.

"The police station's right around here someplace, ain't it?" L.J. asked.

Dub directed him to turn right and turn again onto Exchange Street, and they pulled up in front of a big brick building with white pillars.

L.J. switched off the engine. Staring straight ahead, he said in a flat, dull voice, "All right. Here's where you two take over and I disappear."

Nineteen

"What do you mean, *disappear*?" Allie asked.

L.J. gave a slight shrug. "Go away."

"Where?" Allie asked, feeling totally confused.

"Someplace far from him."

Allie looked at Dub to see if this made any more sense to him than it did to her, but he looked just as bewildered. She turned back to L.J., who was still staring straight ahead, as if into his uncertain future.

"But *where*?" Allie persisted. "You can't just *walk away*." She had an idea. "Where's your mother?"

"Texas," he answered. "I think. I don't know for sure. But that's where she's from, and she always wanted to go back there."

"Can you call her?"

"First thing I gotta do is get away from him."

"You could—" Allie began.

L.J. kept on talking, slowly and deliberately. "I keep thinking, *This time he'll go to jail and I'll be free of him.* But it's always the same. Like in Georgia, he was about to get caught, but we ran off. Then he started up again here. Now he'll drag me off someplace new . . ."

This was by far the most talking L.J. had ever done, and Allie didn't want to interrupt him, even though there were a lot of questions she wanted to ask.

"It'll be the same old thing. He'll read the want ads and get every dog that people are giving away. 'Free to a good home.' " He gave a bitter laugh. "He'll steal some fancy-breed dog like that one belongs to the teacher, if he thinks he can get away with it. He'll call it his moneymaker and say he's about to make big bucks. And then something will happen, just like always—"

L.J. stopped and shook his head angrily. "He just changes the name of his crummy business and starts all over. He thinks he's smart, but if he was so smart we wouldn't have to run away from every place we ever went."

There was a long silence in the cab of the truck, and then L.J. spoke again. Standing up to his father seemed to have released feelings he'd been keeping inside for a long time. "After what happened to Belle at Cutler Creek—"

"Wait a second," Allie interrupted. "Where's Cutler Creek?"

"It's not a place," L.J. answered, sounding tired. "That's just the nice-sounding name the old man gave his business back then: Cutler Creek Kennels."

Allie glanced quickly at Dub. Now they knew what the crossed-out word had been on Mr. Cutler's business card.

"It was a bunch of dogs shut up in plywood cages out in the yard in the blazing sun," L.J. went on. "No creek. No water for miles around unless I carried it out in a bucket."

"What happened there?" Allie asked quietly.

An expression of pain and fury passed over L.J.'s features. He didn't answer the question directly, but kept talking in the same low, tight voice. "After Belle died, Mom couldn't take it anymore. She ran off and took me with her, but we didn't get far. He came and got me. Stole me is more like it. She came for me again, but he got me back." He gave that short, bitter laugh and added, "He always wins. Not that he wants me around, except to do stuff for him."

L.J. had been speaking in a monotone, but his words grew suddenly louder and stronger. "Well, you know what, old man? I can't take it anymore, either. And I'm big enough now to cut out and never have to look at your face again."

He reached for the door handle. When it appeared that he really was about to leave, Allie said, "L.J., wait!"

L.J. turned and his eyes focused on her for the first time since he'd begun talking. His dark eyes looked like two wounds.

Now that she had his attention, Allie didn't know what to say. She wanted to do something to change the awful things she'd just heard, but that was impossible. Nothing in her own life so far had prepared her for this moment. But she had to try something. It seemed like a good time for the truth.

"L.J.," she whispered, "I think Belle knows what a good, brave thing you did tonight."

At the mention of Belle, L.J.'s gaze grew even more intense. "I saw Belle in a dream," Allie continued quickly. "She was in one of those plywood boxes, and she was sad and dirty and sick."

Different emotions passed over L.J.'s face. Allie knew he must have witnessed the scene she had described, and that he had to be wondering how she could have seen it, too.

"I know this sounds crazy, L.J.," Allie said. "But I see ghosts. And I saw Belle."

L.J.'s expression became wary, as if he feared he was being made fun of.

"It's true, L.J.," Dub said quietly.

Allie nodded and hurried on. "They—the ghosts—come to me for help. This is the third time it's happened. And this time, the ghost was a dog. I wasn't sure until now, but it was Belle."

L.J. was listening hard. Allie could see how much he wanted to hear news of Belle, in spite of any doubts he might have about the existence of ghosts.

"When you had Belle, you made a sign for her crate, didn't you?" she asked. "You wrote each letter of her name with a different color crayon. It must have been a few years ago, because the letters looked like a younger kid had written them."

L.J. had the haunted look of someone in the midst of a painful memory. "I was seven," he whispered. "Belle was a great dog. She was *my* dog. She wasn't part of the lousy business. She was so pretty and so smart, you wouldn't believe how smart."

He paused, making a choking sound. Then his eyes narrowed and he continued. "He couldn't stand it. He had to breed her. You shoulda seen her pups. They were so cute. Everybody wanted 'em. He began to make money, more than he'd ever made before. So he kept on breeding her. She needed to rest and get her strength back, but he kept on doing it, until—" He broke off then and looked away.

"L.J.," said Allie, "Belle's ghost came back to stop your father from doing the same thing to other dogs.

She tried in lots of ways to make me see what was going on. But it was hard—I mean, she couldn't talk, and I'd see these terrible pictures, but I couldn't tell what they meant. Then Dub and I thought we'd finally figured out what was going on, but when we came out with the police, your father tricked us. But, tonight—well, don't you see? *You did it*. You stopped him. Now Belle can rest in peace. I feel it. She's gone."

It was true. Now that they had saved the dogs, Belle's ghost was no longer lingering in the world of the living. Her job was finished.

"For real?" L.J. asked in a whisper.

Allie nodded.

L.J. smiled then, a real smile, filled with happiness. And for a moment he, too, seemed to be at peace. But then a shadow of fear passed over his face. "I gotta go," he said, and reached once again for the door handle.

"L.J., no," Allie and Dub both cried at the same time.

"Let's just go inside," Dub urged. "Your father can't hurt you at the *police station*."

"Dub's right, L.J.," pleaded Allie. "Come in with us. We can get this all straightened out. You'll be safe."

"You don't understand," L.J. said in a resigned

voice. "The only safe place for me is far away from him."

"But he's going to be in big trouble," Allie said. "He'll have to go to jail or something, won't he?"

"He's gotten in trouble plenty of times before," L.J. said hopelessly. "And, somehow, he always talks his way out of it. Or there's not quite enough proof of anything to arrest him, or he runs. And then it's just him and me again, and somehow everything was my fault. No way. Not again."

He opened the truck door, jumped down, closed the door, and looked back into the cab. He spoke quickly, saying, "All the towns we been to, I never got to know nobody much. But this place could have been different, maybe." He hesitated, as if there might be more he wanted to say, then shook his head. Looking down, he mumbled, "Sorry about the teacher's dog and all."

He walked a few paces and turned around. "Don't go inside yet, okay? Give me a chance to make tracks outta here."

"Wait, L.J.!" Allie said. "Why don't you take the truck?"

He had broken into a run. Over his shoulder, he called, "Too easy to find me."

A few seconds later, he disappeared.

Twenty

"Are we going to just let him run away?" Allie asked when L.J. was out of sight.

She and Dub looked at each other, frozen with indecision. With each moment that passed, L.J. was farther away, and it was evident that they *were*, indeed, giving him the chance he had asked for.

The puppies in Allie's lap began to cry.

"Poor things," she said. "I bet they're hungry."

A knock on the window next to Dub startled them. "Hey, kids. You all right in there?"

A uniformed policeman was peering through the glass. Dub rolled down the window, and the policeman shone his light on them.

"Yes, sir," Dub answered, squinting in the beam from the flashlight.

"I kept hearing dogs barking out here. What's going on? Who's driving?"

Allie and Dub glanced at each other. Dub murmured, "Here we go."

"It's kind of a long story, Officer," said Allie.

"How many dogs are back there?"

"Ten. Plus these puppies."

"This got anything to do with that wild-goose chase Officer Burke went on earlier?" the policeman asked.

Allie saw Dub's face flush. "Yeah," he mumbled.

The policeman sighed. "All right. Let's go inside." He opened the door of the cab, and Dub and Allie got out. "Whew," he said, wrinkling his nose.

"It's the puppies," Allie explained. "They're not very clean."

With a grimace, the policeman said, "I can see this is going to be one of those nights."

You can say that again, thought Allie.

Inside the station, Allie and Dub related the bare bones of the story. Their parents were called, along with Ed McHugh from the Humane Society and Officer Burke. Both of Dub's parents came. Mr. Nichols came alone, while Allie's mother stayed with Michael.

As Allie and Dub related more and more details about what had happened, the station grew busier and noisier. Phone calls and radio dispatches were made at a frantic pace. A warrant was issued for Mr. Cutler's arrest. Teletypes and faxes including L.J.'s description and that of his father were sent out to every state from New York south. Even though neither L.J. nor his father had more than a half hour's lead, the police had concluded from Allie and Dub's story that either or both of the Cutlers might head south to Texas.

The dogs were loaded into the Humane Society van and taken to the shelter, where, Allie and Dub were told, they'd be cared for and held until L.J.'s father was found and charged.

To Allie's dismay, Hoover was taken, too.

"Just for tonight," Ed McHugh explained. "We'll have a vet check her out thoroughly, and document her condition for the record. You can pick her up in the morning."

It was almost 4 a.m. when Allie and her father got home. "I'm proud of you and Dub," he told her as they headed up the stairs to bed. "And I'm glad you're safe. But tomorrow we're going to have to talk about this business of sneaking out of the house." He kissed her good night and looked at her, his stern expression changing to one of wonder. "I can't believe you *bit* his arm."

Allie laughed. "Neither can I."

She fell into bed and slept, undisturbed by ghosts.

* * *

The next morning, Allie lay in bed, trying to imagine what L.J. was doing at that very moment. Where was he? Had he slept somewhere? Had he caught a ride with someone? Had he eaten? She said a silent prayer that he was safe and on his way to find his mother.

She heard voices and a hammering sound outside in the yard. When she looked out the window, she saw her parents, their neighbor Tom Wright, and Dub's father working together to fence in a portion of the Nicholses' back yard. Michael had made a fort out of the cardboard crate the sections of fence had come in, and was busy playing with his X-Men action figures.

Allie ran down the stairs and into the yard. "What are you guys doing?" she asked.

"Well, honey," said her mother, "we began thinking that we can't have Hoover going back home, not with Mr. Cutler still on the loose. We can't take a chance by leaving her there alone, and we don't want you going over there to take care of her. So your dad was at the building supply store when they opened at seven this morning, and—" She shrugged and gestured to the fence. "She'll have to stay out here because of Michael, but I think she'll be fine until Mr. Henry gets back."

"Thanks, Dad," Allie said. "Thanks, everybody. Can I help?"

Mr. Whitwell handed her a spool of wire and some

wire cutters and told her to cut pieces long enough to twist around the metal poles to hold the fencing in place. She had bent to the task when Michael came over, cupped his hands around her ear, and whispered, "I'm whispering 'cause this is secret."

Allie smiled. "Okay."

"I had a bad dream last night. I came to your room, but you weren't there." He stared accusingly into Allie's eyes.

"I know, Mike. I'm sorry. I was trying to stop the bad things from happening."

Michael nodded wisely. "I thought so. 'Cause the sad noises and the poopy smell are gone."

"I know," Allie said happily.

"Did *you* make them go away?"

"I had help from some friends," she said.

Michael nodded, satisfied, and returned to his fort.

Dub walked across the yard then.

"Hi, Dub!" Allie called. "Where's your bike? Oh, I forgot. At the bean plant, with mine."

"I had to walk all the way over here," Dub said grumpily.

"Poor baby," Mrs. Nichols teased. "You need some breakfast?"

"I had cereal," said Dub. "But thanks."

As they finished up work on the makeshift fence, they talked about what had happened. They were all careful to watch what they said in front of Michael, although he seemed completely occupied with a battle going on among the X-Men in the fort.

Mr. Nichols surprised Allie by saying, "Officer Burke sensed something wrong out at the Cutler house, but—"

Allie couldn't help interrupting. "She did?"

"Yes, but since you didn't find anything in the barn, she couldn't push it. She thought Mr. Cutler's behavior was fishy, though, and that Dub had a good point about the pine scent."

"So she didn't think we were just a couple of stupid kids?" Dub asked.

"Not at all," Mr. Nichols said. "And she said you gave her something, a business card with his former address in Georgia. That helped her look into his past. It turns out Mr. Cutler has a long history of this kind of crime, managing to stay one step ahead of the law and avoiding punishment, just as L.J. said. Also, L.J. missed a lot of school by moving around all the time, and his father had been brought up on charges for that, too, back in Georgia."

Allie looked at Dub. "I bet that's why he made L.J. show up for the last two days of school."

"Probably," Mrs. Nichols agreed.

"Anyway," Allie's father went on, "even before she knew all this, Officer Burke was planning to keep a sharp eye on Mr. Cutler. But she wanted to make sure you two stayed away from him. She thought he was potentially dangerous. And, as you discovered, she was right. There," he added, pounding the last corner pole into place. "For now, we're going to have to just wire the corner shut. I've got to get to work."

"I do, too," said Dub's father. Turning to Dub and Allie, he said, "But first, I want to say that you two had no business sneaking out like that last night."

"It was a very dangerous—and foolish—thing to do," Mrs. Nichols said. "It could have turned out much worse. I don't even like to think of all the things that could have happened to you." Her voice wobbled a little bit, and Allie's father put his arm around her.

"We're going to have to decide what the consequences will be," he said to Allie, and she saw Mr. Whitwell nod in Dub's direction.

Oh well, thought Allie, *at least we're in trouble together.*

"But," Mr. Nichols went on, "even though you broke the rules and were incredibly foolhardy—well, you ended up doing something good, something important. So we'll have to think about your punishment in light of that. Fair enough?"

Allie and Dub nodded.

They were left to finish wiring the fencing to the

poles while the grownups hurried off to get ready for work. Mrs. Nichols said she would take Michael to the baby-sitter's, then drive Allie and Dub to the Humane Society to pick up Hoover.

"Can I trust you two to stay here today with Hoover while I'm at the store?" she asked.

"Yes, Mom," Allie said sheepishly. Dub nodded.

"No daring rescues? No slipping off to solve a crime better left to the police?"

"No, Mom. Honest."

"All right."

Later, when Hoover had been given a clean bill of health by the vet, they brought her back to Allie's house. Mrs. Nichols made them promise again that they would stay put and behave themselves, and she went to work. Allie and Dub brought the hose around to the back yard, filled Michael's plastic kiddy pool, and gave Hoover a bubble bath. They spent the day in the fenced-in yard with her, playing catch and teaching her to balance a bone on her nose, hoping to make her forget her kidnapping and the hours she had spent in the bean plant.

"She seems just like her old self, don't you think?" Allie asked.

"Like nothing ever happened," agreed Dub.

But a lot *had* happened, and continued to happen. For one thing, Allie and Dub were both grounded for a week. It wasn't too bad, they decided, because they were allowed to use the phone and the computer. They were supposed to be thinking about how dangerous their middle-of-the-night escapade had been, but what they mostly talked and thought and wondered about was L.J. and his father and Belle.

The day their confinement ended, they learned from Officer Burke that Mr. Cutler had been caught and was going to be prosecuted. They learned, too, that L.J. had made it to Texas and found his mother. Officer Burke said Mrs. Cutler had been trying for years to track her son down and get him back, but Mr. Cutler had always managed to elude her. She'd hounded the police and hired private detectives, and had just about run out of money and hope when L.J. showed up on her doorstep.

Everyone was happy with this news, but Allie and Dub longed to know more. Then, a week later, a letter with a Texas postmark arrived at Allie's house. The address read only "Ally Nickels, Seneca, New York." Luckily, it was enough. Allie opened the letter, her hands trembling eagerly.

Dear Miss Fix-it (ha ha kidding) and your boyfriend (kidding again),

I am in Texas. Bet you never thought I'd make it. Mom and me heard from the police that they caught the old man. They said he can't take me from here, especially since this time he is really going to jail.

I hope the dogs are okay and are at good homes for real now. I remember what you said about Belle, that she is at peace. I am getting a dog. I am naming her Seneca for where you live.

Yours truly,
Lamar James Cutler

"*Lamar?*" Dub said when Allie read the letter to him over the phone.

"That's what it says."

"Wow, I can't believe he wrote us a letter."

"I know. He sounds good, don't you think?"

"Yeah, being with his mom and getting a new dog and all."

"So you want to come over? We can write back."

"Be there in a minute."

When Dub arrived, they sat at the picnic table on the back porch with a pencil and tablet.

"This'll be our rough draft," Allie said.

Dub laughed. "Mr. Henry would be so proud."

Their final draft said:

Dear Lamar,

It was great to get your letter! It's good you found your mom and are getting a dog! We wondered about you all the time and whether you were sleeping outside and eating berries and stuff. It's amazing you got so far, all the way to Texas.

We were both grounded after that night. Our parents were pretty mad, but also kind of happy about the way it turned out. Everybody was worried about you. They're glad you're okay and so are we.

Mr. Henry's dog, Hoover, is fine. Some of the other dogs were adopted, but some are still waiting. Mr. Henry could hardly believe everything that happened. He said he had a feeling about you that you were really nice, and if you ask us, he was right.

The pet store is Closed Until Further Notice while they investigate the owner lady, Enid. Our friend James worked there and he told us that she didn't take good care of the puppies and a lot of them got sick and died. She's in trouble, but not as much as your father.

It's all because of what you did. Belle must be smiling up in Dog Heaven!

We hope you come back to visit or maybe we'll come to Texas sometime. Tell us when you get Seneca and we will send her some of our healthy dog biscuits!

Your friends,

Allie Nichols and Dub Whitwell

P.S. Write back soon.